ATTENTION R

P9-DNV-996

Did you love this book?

Booksellers	Readers
Recommend it for Indie Next!	Rate it on Goodreads!
indienextlist@bookweb.org	goodreads.com

We love bloggers and hope you'll share this book with your readers early and often, but request that full reviews get posted as close to the publication month as possible. Thank you!

Publicity Contact: Eva_Zimmerman@chroniclebooks.com
Foreign Rights Contact: subrights@chroniclebooks.com

All prices and plans are subject to change.
Find more distinctive books at chroniclekids.com.

chronicle books · san francisco

ADVANCE READER'S COPY

TITLE:	Benbee and the Teacher Griefer
AUTHOR:	K.A. Holt
ISBN:	978-1-4521-8251-3
PRICE:	$17.99
TRIM SIZE:	$5^5/_8$ x $8^1/_8$ inches
PAGES:	348
AGES:	8–12
GRADES:	4 and up
GENRE:	Middle Grade
PUBLICATION DATE:	SEPTEMBER 2020

TO PLACE ORDERS in the U.S., please contact your Chronicle Books sales representative, e-mail order.desk@hbgusa.com, or call customer service toll-free at 800-759-0190.

chroniclekids.com

The Kids Under the Stairs

BenBee

and the Teacher Griefer

by K.A. HOLT

chronicle books•san francisco

A very special thank you to Christy Stallop, fine artist and friend. Christy creates delightful paintings and sculptures of luchador grackles that you can find all over Austin, Texas (and beyond). When I asked Christy if one of my characters could represent himself as a luchador grackle, she graciously agreed without hesitation. My renderings don't come close to Christy's playful energy and skillful talent, so it was extra kind of her to allow me to borrow her ingenious idea. You can find Christy's work all over Austin, from galleries to billboards to murals to towering eight feet over the grounds of the Austin Public Library. You can also find her work online at **www.christystallop.com**. Javier and I thank you to the moon and back, Christy!

Library of Congress Cataloging-in-Publication Data available.

ISBN 978-1-4521-8251-3

Design by Jennifer Tolo Pierce.
Typeset in Fedra Mono and Cultura New.

10 9 8 7 6 5 4 3 2 1

Chronicle Books LLC
680 Second Street
San Francisco, California 94107

Chronicle Books—we see things differently. Become part of our community at **www.chroniclekids.com**.

FOR CHRISTINE BURROUGHS:

*an enigma, a force of nature, and the reason
why I will always recognize prepositions as
something a squirrel can do to a tree.*

Grade 6 Exit Level

Florida Rigorous Aca[...]
Summary Report—Langu[...]

Benjamin Hobart Bellows

English Lan[...]

	1	2	3	4
Basic Understanding				
Comprehension of Literary Elements	x			
Analysis and Evaluation	x			
Understanding of and Correct Use of Grammar and Punctuation		x		

Writng Assessment

	1	2	3	4
Writes Explanatory Texts	x			
Writes Narrative Texts	x			
Writes Persuasive Texts	x			
Comprehension of Purpose and Audience		x		
Plans and Revises to Strengthen Text	x			

Did NOT meet STANDARDS

KEY	
4	Exceeds Standards
3	Meets Standards
2	Working Toward Standards
1	Not Meeting Standards
N/A	Not Assessed

SEMESTER COMMENTS

Recommendations:

- Summer school remediation
- Retake Language Arts Assessment

handwritten note:

* highly intelligent
* works hard, lacks focus
* possible dysgraphia
— why no 504?

Grade 6 Exit Level

Florida Rigorous Academic Assessment Test
Summary Report—Language Arts Test Performance

Benita Sol Ybarra

English Language Arts

	1	2	3	4
Basic Understanding		x		
Comprehension of Literary Elements		x		
Analysis and Evaluation		x		
Understanding of and Correct Use of Grammar and Punctuation		x		

Writng Assessment

	1	2	3	4
Writes Explanatory Texts		x		
Writes Narrative Texts		x		
Writes Persuasive Texts		x		
		x		
		x		

+ dyslexia diagnosed in grade 2

+ inquisitive to the point of distraction (sometimes)

+ natural leader ☆

SEMESTER COMMENTS

ecommendations:

Summer school remediation

Retake Language Arts Assessment

1	Not Meeting Standards
N/A	Not Assessed

Grade 6 Exit Level

Florida Rigorous Academic Assessment Test

Summary Report—Langua...

Jordan Jackson

English La...

Basic Understanding
Comprehension of Literary Elements
Analysis and Evaluation
Understanding of and Correct Use of Grammar and Punctuation

ADHD diagnosis at age 4

KINETIC learner

kind, funny, everyone's friend :)

Writng Assessment

	1	2	3	4
Writes Explanatory Texts	x			
Writes Narrative Texts		x		
Writes Persuasive Texts	x			
Comprehension of Purpose and Audience		x		
Plans and Revises to Strengthen Text	x			

Did NOT meet STANDARDS

SEMESTER COMMENTS

Recommendations:

- Summer school remediation
- Retake Language Arts Assessment

KEY	
4	Exceeds Standards
3	Meets Standards
2	Working Toward Standards
1	Not Meeting Standards
N/A	Not Assessed

| Basic Underst: |
| Comprehensic |
| Analysis and F |
| Understanding
Grammar and |

| Writes Explan: |
| Writes Narrati |
| Writes Persuas |
| Comprehensic |
| Plans and Rev: |

District Memo

Javier Julio Jimenez
Age: 12
Grade: (entering) 7th

* previously homeschooled out of state

* parent-reported disfluency

* no previous standardized testing,
  no accredited grades

* summer school recommended, for student
  assessment prior to beginning of school year

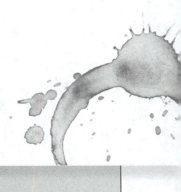

KEY	
4	Exceeds Standards
3	Meets Standards
2	Working Toward Standards
1	Not Meeting Standards
N/A	Not Assessed

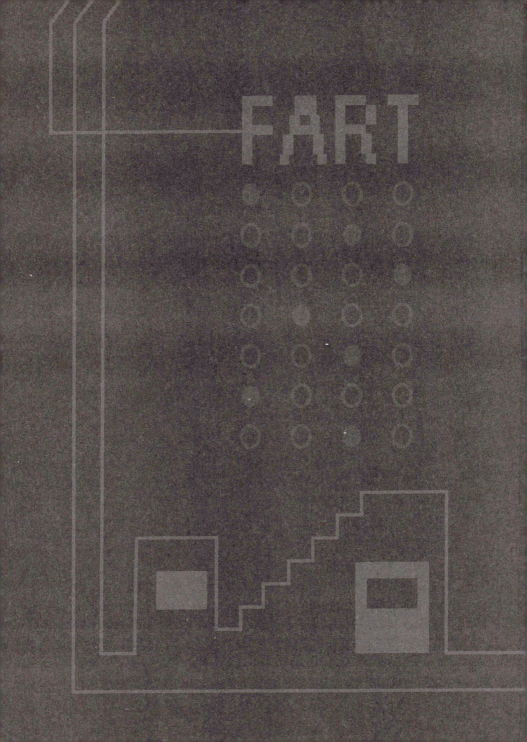

<Part I>

SAVE UR SERVER

IT'S TIME TO SAVE UR SERVER, SAVE UR SELF!

Hello! Welcome to your own curated Sandbox adventure! As you move through your journey, you will be faced with many choices. Will you opt for adventure and danger, or will you choose certainty and likely, though not guaranteed (watch out for those sneaky ghosts!), safety? Who will be your allies? Who will be your foes? Be careful! Sometimes it's hard to figure out one from the other.

So!   *BUTTNERDS*

Are you ready for your adventure to begin? Great! What would you like to name your server?

DINOSMOS!

Dingleberries   *Dinosmos!*

GHOSTKILLER VIPS

Fairy Farmers

Congratulations! You have created a unique and impressive name for your server. Now you have a big choice to make:

To allow anyone to play on your server, turn to **page 15**.

To password protect your server for invited players only, turn to **page 9**.

From *Save Ur Server, Save Ur Self: A Many Choices Sandbox Adventure Book* by Tennessee Williamson

BEN B.

<BenBee>

I don't like to read.
There.
I said it.

□ □ □ □

Books have too many words.
It takes forever to read a page.
It takes at least infinity to read
    a chapter.
This is why

shhh

I have never
and will never
finish reading a book.

□ □ □ □

It's not that I hate words.
I don't.
It's not that I hate stories.
I don't.
It's not even that I hate books.
I don't.
It's just . . .
I don't like to read.
It's hard to read.

When you're in first grade,
pretty much *everyone* has a
    hard time reading.
In second grade,
lots of kids still have a
    hard time.
But then,
in third
fourth
fifth
sixth
the other kids,
they figure it out.

And when you don't?
It's just . . .
Uuuuuuuugh.

□ □ □ □

You know what's not
uuuuugh??
You know what always makes
    sense?
(And when it doesn't, is
actually fun to figure out?)
You know what has zero
    words?

You know what's the opposite
of boring?

Sandbox.

With every minute I can spare,
I build universes.
I lead alliances.
I save the world.
Me.
I do that.
Without reading a word.

▫ ▫ ▫ ▫

The thing is,
unlike *other* things,
you can't fail at Sandbox

It's a fail-free zone.
Mistakes become inventions.
Accidents become lessons.

You don't just imagine the
impossible.
You make it happen.
You bring it to life.

So tell me this:
if I spend every day

bringing the impossible
    to life,
then why can't I figure out
how to pass the dang FART?

▫ ▫ ▫ ▫

Florida
Rigorous
Academic
Assessment
Test

Everyone calls it the FART,
even though
even *I* know
that's not how you spell fart.

This class,
You know who we are?
We're the FART Failures.

*Dang, son, you have FART
    Failure again?
Only cure for that is
    summer school.
If you work hard.
Can you work hard?*

▫ ▫ ▫ ▫

How did I even fail the FART
      to begin with?
We spent so many days last year
practicing
studying
practicing more.
Filling the bubbles
carefully
perfectly
no marks
out of line.
But something *was* out of line.
My brain, I guess.
Because even after all of that
I still failed it.
My sharp pencil a torpedo
sinking that test
to the bottom
of all the other tests,
drowning
in so many
bubbles.

▫ ▫ ▫ ▫

At least I'm not drowning
all alone.

Jordan J.
Javier.
Ben Y.
Ben B. ←-- that's me

Ms. Jackson.
Summer school.
Language Arts.
Room 113.

All working
all summer
to keep our heads
above
this bubbly
FART water.

▫ ▫ ▫ ▫

Room 113
is not even a room
at all.

You go through double doors
to get to the stairs
and then
you don't go up those—
you go around them
and then under them.

Four desks
crammed in the stairwell,
a table for Ms. J,
a whiteboard on an easel.

Make your Harry Potter jokes.
We've heard them all.

□ □ □ □

Oh, Benjamin.
Again?
Why do you keep failing?

Dad's words
turned to icy, stabby
spikes that still
live in my brain.

I hear those words
when I wake up
when I'm in class
when I eat lunch
when I go to bed.

Fail.

Sometimes it shimmers in
       the air,
so bright
I can almost see it
dancing and laughing at me.
Pointing at and taunting me.
Because it knows,
just like I know
that I did work hard.
I do work hard.
And it's never enough.
Never is.
Never has been.
Never will be.

How do my parents not
       see that?
It's like their eyes are so wide,
looking for so many ways
I can be better and smarter,
they can't actually see
what's right in front of them:

There is no better.
There is no smarter.
This is as good as Ben B gets.
This is just . . . who I am.

□ □ □ □

Except!

When I click on my screen,
dive into Sandbox,
become BenBee
instead of Ben B . . .
when I am cloaked in yellow
    and black,
I actually do a good job.
Every day.
I build and create.
I learn and remember.
When I am BenBee
instead of Ben B.
I am
the best me.
I am
the smart me.

Why can't BenBee be the
    real me?
Why can't BenBee be the one
    my parents see?

□ □ □ □

Why can't school be like
    Sandbox?
No instructions.
No manuals.
You just try stuff.
Sometimes it works
and you make a volcano
to protect your private island.
Sometimes it doesn't work
and you accidentally make a
    waterfall
out of chickens.
See?
Even when it doesn't work,
it's still fun.

(And, you know?
I guess I learn stuff, too.)

□ □ □ □

Jordan laughed so hard
when I told him about my
    chickenfall
he fell
right out of his desk,
a Jordanfall.

□ □ □ □

You know,
Ben Y said,
turning around in her chair,
a chickenfall
is the most divergent idea
I've heard
in years.

□ □ □ □

Everyone laughed at that.

□ □ □ □

About one million times a day
Ms. J tells us:
You're the smartest kids in
this school.
You are divergent thinkers.
Divergent thinkers change
the world.

Mm-hmm.
I'm sure all the world-
changers
had summer school
classrooms
under the stairs.

□ □ □ □

Today, though, Ms. J
sounds like she's got popcorn
stuck
in her throat.

She *ahem-ahems.*
She *ahem-ahems* again,
while we all laugh at Jordanfalls
and divergent chickens.

I can see that you all have
a lot to talk about
right now,
but when I ask
questions
about the reading,
everyone is silent.
Why is that?

□ □ □ □

That's because none of us
do the reading.
It's boring.
And terrible.

I don't say that.
But maybe I should.

□ □ □ □

She seems so hopeful.
It kind of makes me sad.
But mostly it makes me mad.
I don't need to disappoint
      anyone else
in my life.
I don't need to watch the light
dim in their eyes
when they figure out
what I can't do.

▫ ▫ ▫ ▫

I can't *do* a lot of things.
Even though I'm always busy
trying to do All Of The Things.

Tune up those fine motors skills,
Mom says,
with art classes!

Strengthen those gross
      motor skills,
learn teamwork,
be social,
Dad says,
by playing soccer!

Pass the FART,
Mom says,
tutoring will help!

Handwriting practice,
Dad says,
will complement those
      art lessons!

And music,
Mom says,
music activates your brain
      in such
important ways.
Don't forget music!

So.

Art Class Monday.
Soccer Practice Tuesday.
FART Tutoring Wednesday.
Handwriting Thursday.
Piano Lessons Friday.
Soccer Game Saturday.
House Cleaning Sunday.

All of this
extra
bonus
helpful
learning
is so exhausting,
my brain mostly wants to
hide in a corner
of my mind
and think about chickenfalls
until *I* fall
asleep.

□ □ □ □

Now that I think about it,
all of my extracurriculars
make a weird thing happen:
even with . . .
the reading,
the tests,
the failing,
the struggling,
the blah blah blah,
the same same same,
sometimes school's like

a dang
vacation
from everything else
in my
lined-up,
signed-up,
piled-up,
minivan
on the way
backseat burger
can't be late
here and there
never good enough
never smart enough
everyday
life.

Dad wants me to
practice this,
study that,
listen up,
never quit,
Do you hear me, Benjamin?
Do I need to take away your
screens, Benjamin?

But even when I
practice
study
listen
never quit,

Even when I
try to read better
try to pass every test
try to win win win

Dad never says,
good job.
He never says,
nice try.
The look in his eye
only ever dims
instead of brightens.
So maybe summer school
isn't so bad.
Maybe it's actually a break
from the summer vacation
I could have had,
disappointing Mom and Dad.
Maybe it's a chance
to finally get better
at something
even if that something

is just
getting away
from them.

That's a weird thing to think,
right?

□ □ □ □

A screechy noise
snaps me back
to the stairwell.

What can I dooooooo?

Ms. J throws her arms in
        the air.
Very dramatic.

*What can I do to get you
        to read?*
This is important.

She taps the book on
        Javier's desk.

It's required.
No one
in this class

can fail
the Assessment
again,
you hear me?
Do you want me to yell?
Do you want me to fail you?

She takes a deep breath.
She looks up at the underbelly
 of the stairs,
the zigzag lid to our too-
 tight space,
as if the answers are written
 there.

This class was created
for divergent learners . . .
just for you!
To help you,
not to punish you.
But you all have to help me, too.

Now.

Can anyone tell me about
 the reading?

No?

Her mouth scrunches up.
She smacks the book onto
 her desk.
BAM.

Get out your spelling lists.

□ □ □ □

I think what Ms. J doesn't
 understand,
what she totally
totally
doesn't get
is this:
the FART Failures?
We still fail even when we
 do try.
So why not skip the
 frustrating part?
When we can just stay
 at zero?

BEN Y

<0benwhY>

They're renovating the
   teachers' restrooms.

Ms. J's mouth—
a tight line.
Her dangly earrings
quiver.

This means teachers must use
   the student restrooms.

Her breath comes in short
   bursts.
The tops of her ears glow
   bright red.

And THAT means, I found
   this.

She holds up a sopping
   wet book.
It shakes in her hand,
matching the quiver
of her earrings,
a danse
macabre
that maybe
might just

have something
possibly
to do with
me.

Uh-oh.
Uh-oh.
UH-OH.

I found it,
she repeats,
lurching toward me,
In a toilet.

Ms. J slams the book,
really slams it,
on my desk.

I mean,
she basically *throws* it.
At me.

▫ ▫ ▫ ▫

We are paused.
Like the middle of a game,
when you need to
stop,

strategize,
organize,
fall back,
breathe.

Think, self,
think.
Should I tell her it's not
    my book?
Even though I'm the only
    girl in class?
And it's pretty obvious the
    only girl
would be the one
to flush a book
in the girls' restroom?

Should I mention that maybe
gender-neutral bathrooms
would be useful
in the future
for a variety of reasons
(not just because
gender assumptions
ratted me out
in this particular situation)?

Should I tell her it fell out
    of my backpack?
Should I tell her someone
    stole it?
Should I act grateful to have
    it back?
Should I just stay quiet?

□ □ □ □

One million seconds go past.
Ms. J stays paused
right here
in front of my desk.

A tiny bit of splashed
toilet
water
(grossssssss)
drips
from my chin
(omgggggggg)
onto my fabulous
floral
button-down
I found
for two dollars
at Stardust thrift.
(arghhhhhhhh)

Then.
Boom.
The world unpauses.

Jordan J whistles,
low,
long,
an up-down noise
that we all know means
what the what just happened.

Ms. J's angry face
melts back to her regular face,
and then to a surprised face.

Oh my gosh.
Benita.
I'm sorry.
I didn't mean to—
And her hands cross under
    her arms,
as if her armpits can prevent
another wet book
from flying out
and everyone is
so
so
quiet,

like sitting-at-a-funeral quiet
and
you can hear
the drip
drip
of the toilet water
slipping from the book
across my desk
and onto the floor,
and everyone's eyes
flash
from her
to me
to the book
and back again,
an infinite loop
in desperate need
of a reboot,
a ctrl-alt-del
so we can take a new path
so we can start this moment
all over again.

▫ ▫ ▫ ▫

We all have bad days.
I appear to be having one
right now,

but,
bless
your
heart,
Benita. . . .

Why,
why,
why would you try
to flush
a book?

▫ ▫ ▫ ▫

I don't really think she means
    bless your heart,
Jordan J whispers to me.
I think she means that instead
    of a swear.

I give him a look that
definitely
means a swear.

He stops whispering.

▫ ▫ ▫ ▫

The thing is . . .
some girl,
I don't even know who,
was at the sinks
while I was in the stall
and she said,
You know that tall girl?
The one who always wears
    red lipstick?

And my heart sped up,
because that tall girl
with the red lips
is definitely me.

Another girl said,
Yeah,
like she was super bored,
and the first girl said,
I saw her walking into the
    Dummy Potter class.
You know,
the one under the stairs?
And she had, like,
a copy of The Horse and
    the Mouse

in her hand,
and didn't we read that in, like,
third grade?

The bored girl said,
Well, maybe it's a Baby
    Potter class
and not a Dummy Potter class.
Maybe they're babies in
    big-kid bodies?
I don't know.
Who cares?

I could hear the shrug in
    her voice,
and I don't know why,
but that shrug
set me on fire.

My guts burned,
my face burned,
my brain burned
as it tried to not remember
the mahogany voice
reading me *The Horse and*
    the Mouse,
when I was a third grader;
the mahogany voice

that used to read me so
    many books;
the mahogany voice
I haven't heard
in almost
exactly
one year.

I didn't want to think about
    his voice.
I didn't want the sadness to
    wash over me,
to drown me,
to choke me,
so I guess I tried to wash
away the book,
drown the memory,
choke down the feelings,
and I pushed it
shoved it
crushed it
drowned it,
in the toilet
furthest
(farthest?)
from the door.

I flushed,
flushed,
flushed,
until the water poured out,
flushed more
and more,
trying to flush the Horse,
trying to flush the Mouse,
trying to flush
the memories,
the questions,
the voice,
the Whys,
flush them all
all
all
alllllllllllllllll
away.

□ □ □ □

Of course I don't say
any of this
out loud
right now
in class.

Sometimes too much to say
becomes nothing to say
because, just like nothing,
too much has no beginning
or end.

□ □ □ □

Ms. J keeps looking at me
as if I crushed her heart
like a baby toe
against the corner
of a dang
coffee table.

No.
Her look is worse than
        a crushed toe.
Her crumpled face,
even while she tries
to be calm now,
looks like the book was
        her family,
made of her own blood,
and I tried to kill it,
with my own dirty

bare
hands.

I mean, *who* loves a book
    that much?

  □ □ □ □

I close my eyes.
I imagine Ms. J is a ghost
    in Sandbox.
She's shimmering,
ready to slime me.

Benita.

Answer me.

Why
    did
        you
            do
                this?

I look away.
Where is Ghostkiller when
    you need him?

My insides fill with cold
    ghost slime.
Some of it oozes out of
    my eyes.

  □ □ □ □

Ma'am?
Can you please stop calling
    me Benita?
That isn't my name anymore.

It's Ben.

Ben Y.

I sniff,
try to delete
the ghost slime
from my cheeks.

I hate that
my voice sounds small.
I hate that
I feel just as small.

Do you know?

How it feels?
To fail the FART?

I don't mention
that it's
maybe
very
possible
I failed on purpose.

Do you know?
How it feels?
To be forced to take
     summer school?

I don't mention
that I
maybe
possibly
have been actually
looking forward to it.
A distraction.
A place to spend my days
that's not my house.

Do you know?
How it feels?

When you're forced to read
     a book written for babies
and you still can't do it?

I don't mention how,
when I see those words,
I hear the mahogany voice;
that it haunts me,
that I've spent the last year
desperate to hear it
and desperate to *not* hear it.
I don't mention that I can't
     read the book
because the words swim
but also because the
     words hurt.

Do you?

□ □ □ □

Ms. J kneels by my desk,
her giant hair a coconut-
smelling cloud
blocking out the stairwell light.
She takes the wet book.
She stands up.

Everyone,
she says,
follow me.

▫ ▫ ▫ ▫

Are we even allowed
to go outside
in the middle
of the school day?

Why?
Why?
Why is Ms. J
breaking so many
rules
today?

All the other eyes
looking at mine
are asking
why
why
why,
too.

Her caftan,
like a sheet in the wind,
billows after her,
as she moves quickly
and we follow,
but not close enough
to get tripped up
in all the ripples
of her epic dress.

Where
are
we
going?

▫ ▫ ▫ ▫

I guess we're going here,
under the giant willow tree.

I guess we're sitting in the dirt.

I guess we're staring at
    each other.

I guess we're staring at her.

Dare I even ask
the simplest
and most obvious
question:

Why?
In the world?
Are we here?

▫ ▫ ▫ ▫

*In Japan there is a practice
    called forest bathing.*

Ms. J's voice is soft,
almost a whisper,
blending with the soft
almost-whispers
of the tree.

*It means calmly walking
    around in a forest
until you feel relaxed and
    rejuvenated.
It helps you think clearer.
It helps you feel better.*

*We don't have a forest here
    at school,
so this tree will have to do.
Can we all sit for a few
minutes
until I—
until we feel calmer?*

Jordan J makes a fart noise.

*Jordan,
if that is what calms you,
I ask that you go do it in the
    restroom.*

Jordan J doesn't move,
but he whispers,
It's Jordan J, actually.

And Ben B whispers back
    to him,
Why the J, dude?

And Jordan whispers,
*If you're Ben B and Ben Y
    is Ben Y,*

And Ms J is Ms J shouldn't
    I be Jordan J?
Otherwise people will be—
ENOUGH
Ms. J shouts.

She closes her eyes,
then, in a much quieter voice,
says,
Can we please,
please
silently reflect
for just one moment?

We all sit under the tree.
Quietly.
But our eyes bounce around,
silently saying,

What is happening?
while Ms. J sits with *her*
    eyes closed
for a very
very
long time.

▫ ▫ ▫ ▫

Is my teacher going bonkers
    bananas?
Because I tried to flush
    my book?

JORDAN J

<JordanJmageddon!!!!>

Everyone was so serious I had to make a fart noise, it's just a thing that had to be done and I don't know why we're all under this tree, but it's super weird especially after Ms. J (no relation) threw that book like WHAM I mean, can't you get fired for doing something like that? Can you? I don't think *anyone* is allowed to throw books, teachers or students. Oh my gosh it sounded like I just said no one is allowed to throw teachers or students, which I'm pretty sure is totally true, but is not what I meant. Haha. I'm like a poet or something. The thing is, though, Benita, I mean, Ben Y is totally right about the book being for babies or whatever. It is and I wish I'd thought to flush mine, too, though I guess it didn't work very well when she tried it and now we're all here and Ms. J seems extra super freaked out that she freaked out and what is even happening.

▫ ▫ ▫ ▫

I mean, I'm not going to make another fart noise, but I'm going to think about it.

▫ ▫ ▫ ▫

I heard some of everyone talking about a chickenfall and I have never heard of a chickenfall, so I had to try to laser pinpoint my mind on their conversation in order to figure out what the heck they were talking about. Turns out, they were talking about Sandbox which is a game I love love love, so today, before the bell I was all, *Hey you guys, talk to me about your chickenfalls, because it sounds maybe even better than the swingset I made where the swings are pigs.* Everyone looked at me like *I* was a pig swing for a minute and then Ben Y said *Hold up, you're JordanJmageddon!!!!* and I was like of course, and she was all, *Well well.* And then everyone except for the quiet guy said our avatar names and holy dang this is like a class full of famous people, especially Ben B, holy cow I saw him play at SBCon4 last year and he is legit legit, like if he had been there in real life and not just in the VIP server, playing on the big widescreen, he could've like signed autographs on people's *faces* I bet.

□ □ □ □

Like, everyone in this class loves Sandbox times a million and we all were talking so fast and at the same time it got super loud and Ms. J said, *I wish you guys could get as excited about reading as you do about video games,* and everyone laughed and was like, *Noooooo waaaayyyy,* and even the quiet kid who didn't say his avatar name cause he was drawing something that took one hundred and ten percent of his concentration, even he laughed and he never usually makes a noise at all ever, he just draws or stares hard in front of his desk like he wants to be invisible or shoot lasers out of his eyes. Or play Sandbox. I bet everyone in the whole world plays Sandbox. Well, everyone except for my dog Spartacus because she's a dog and except for my mom who is a mom and who kind of hates Sandbox, but I bet she'd like it if she'd ever play with me, which she won't because she is just so busy, Jordan, she has so much to do all the time, Jordan, can't you just turn that off for a second and PUT AWAY YOUR SOCKS?!?!?!

▫ ▫ ▫ ▫

Actually, probably Ms. J doesn't play Sandbox either. So. Two people in the whole world. Ms. J and my mom. Well, and Spartacus, who is not a person, but is the smartest dog in the history of ever, so basically a person, but better. So, like two-point-five people in the whole world don't play Sandbox.

▫ ▫ ▫ ▫

Also, Spartacus is a girl, just to be clear, not a boy like in the movie not that it really matters because she's brave and strong and protects me like the other Spartacus would if he knew me or if I lived in that movie which he doesn't and I don't.

▫ ▫ ▫ ▫

Ms. J is talking now so I guess the quiet part under the tree is done, so that's good because I don't do super great at quiet parts anywhere. I'm a mover and a shaker and a talker and a mover-some-more-er at least that's what my mom says. She says it isn't bad it's just different than most people. I guess I kind of like how Ms. J says we're all divergent thinkers, because I am a divergent everything-er. I have a million ideas a day that sometimes get in the way of my other million ideas so I have to stare out the window for a little bit while all the ideas bang into each other. PS it turns out when you have to stare out the window for a little bit or a lotta bit that it isn't super great for taking the FART because all of a sudden your time is over and you aren't finished and you find yourself in summer school sitting under a tree not making fart noises even though you really, really want to.

□ □ □ □

Wait. What did Ms. J just say? Something about changing books? Cool, cool, no more baby books, except if the baby book is hard to read then I'm not sure another book would actually be better? *Can we just choose to not read?*

Ooh. I said that last part out loud. Oops.

Answer: No.

Not surprising.

□ □ □ □

Wait. What did Ms. J just say? Rewind, brain, try to listen again . . . blah blah blah . . . she's going to choose a better book and also she wants us to help her help us. She's leaning forward like she has a secret and we're all leaning forward and we're still under this tree and today has been a strange day.

Help me help you read.

Ms. J is saying that to each one of us and we are all staring at her like she needs some hot chocolate and a quiet corner because I'm pretty sure she's crazy and when my mom yells, *You're making me feel crazy, Ben!* she always likes hot chocolate and a quiet corner.

JAVIER

<JaJaJavier:)>

1) WHAT EVEN IS THIS PLACE???
   (FRESHWATER, FL? TRY FINDING THAT ON A MAP!)

2) HOW DID I GET HERE???
   (WHO JUST QUITS THEIR JOB AND MOVES CROSS-COUNTRY? OTHER THAN -YOU, MOM???)

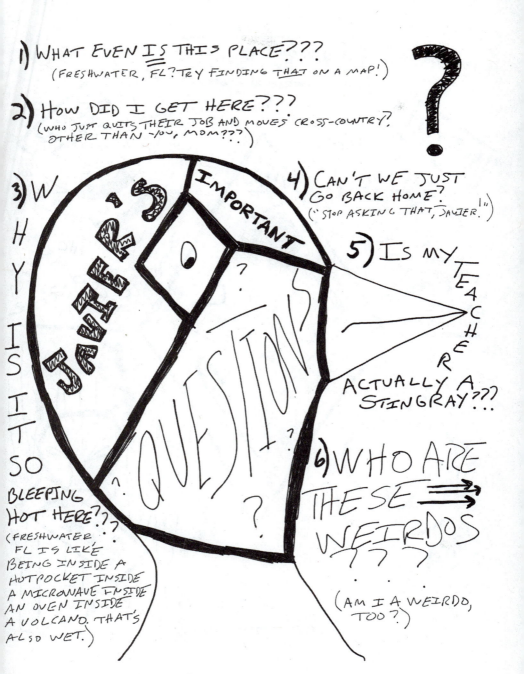

3) WHY IS IT SO BLEEPING HOT HERE???
   (FRESHWATER FL IS LIKE BEING INSIDE A HOTPOCKET INSIDE A MICROWAVE INSIDE AN OVEN INSIDE A VOLCANO. THAT'S ALSO WET.)

JAVIER'S

IMPORTANT

QUESTIONS

4) CAN'T WE JUST GO BACK HOME?
   ("STOP ASKING THAT, JAVIER!")

5) IS MY TEACHER ACTUALLY A STINGRAY???...

6) WHO ARE THESE ⇒⇒ WEIRDOS ???
   (AM I A WEIRDO, TOO?)

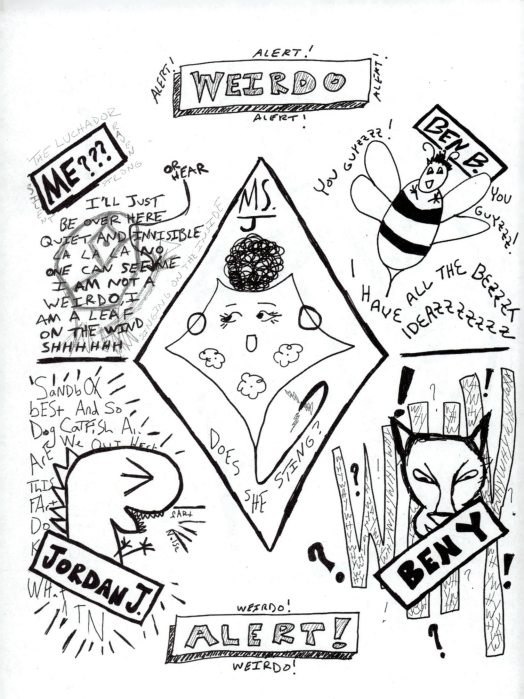

40

BEN B

<BenBee>

I'm listening as she says:

Help me
help you
read

to the whole class,
one by one,
branch to branch
face to face,
and I want to laugh
because it's weird, right?
All of it.
Right now.
Like a dream you have
when your fever is sky-high
and your mom says,
Hmmm?
No, Benjamin.
That's not an alligator.
That's your sister.

It's weird.

But Ms. J?
She keeps saying
help me
help you
read
and instead of laughing,
now I'm wondering,
What *could* she do?
How *could* she help me?
How *could* I help her help me?
Could that even be a thing?
Maybe?

If I could finally be
a good, smart reader,
that would mean
dealing with one less thing.

Dealing with one less thing
would give me more time
for my favorite thing.

And that is a thing
I am in favor of.

▫ ▫ ▫ ▫

See what I did there?
I drew a line,
a string,
from worst to best,
if *that*, then *this*.

If I read better,
then I can play Sandbox more.

See?
I'm no dummy.

▫ ▫ ▫ ▫

Put a book in Sandbox,
I say.
That might make me read.

▫ ▫ ▫ ▫

OrRuinSandbox,
Jordan J says,
smashing the words together,
pretending they're a cough.

▫ ▫ ▫ ▫

You can't put a book in
    Sandbox, silly.

Ben Y shakes her head,
but her eyes
flash
meteor bright
and lock on to mine.

▫ ▫ ▫ ▫

We type in Sandbox,
I say.
That's almost like a book.

I look at Ben Y,
she looks at me,
a triangle of thinking.

▫ ▫ ▫ ▫

You have to read a real book,
    you guys.
You can't just play games and
    call it a book.

Ms. J looks up,
searching out the blue sky
between the swaying fronds
of the tree.

□ □ □ □

What if we read a real book
and you play Sandbox and we
see what real books are like
and you see that Sandbox
isn't just a game you PLAY,
which is frankly offensive, if
you ask me.

□ □ □ □

Wait.
Yes!
Jordan J is on to something.

□ □ □ □

What if,
I say,
for every one minute we read,
Ms. J plays
one minute of Sandbox?

Ben Y's meteor stare
explodes into a smile.

Javier's eyes
go wide wide wide,
anime-style.

Jordan J points at me.
THAT is what I said, Buzzy
Ben. Yasss. She won't be a
teacher griefer . . . right?
We'll teach her.

My heart beats faster.
She'll teach us.
She'll learn it's more than
        a game.
We'll learn . . . to, uh,
        read better.
All teaching. No griefing.

□ □ □ □

Ms. J's crinkle face looks
        just like
my sister Janie's crinkle face
when Mom says something like
Did you know they make
organic Pop-Tarts?

Ms. J crinkles more, says,

*I don't think we can play video
    games in class, Ben.*

But her crinkles soften
just barely,
just carefully enough,
the tiniest smile
in the history of smiles,
peeking around the crinkles,
just like Janie
when she tastes the organic
    Pop-Tart
and realizes
it's still actually junk food.

▫ ▫ ▫ ▫

If Ms. J eats the Sandbox
    Pop-Tart,
then she'll realize it's
good
and
good for you.
(Sort of.)

▫ ▫ ▫ ▫

If Ms. J realizes Sandbox is
    good
and good for you,
maybe she'll also realize:
it's smart
it makes *me* smart.
it makes the *whole class* smart.

And that's what she wants,
    right?
For us to be smart?

If we're smart,
we will all pass the FART
    retake.

So clearly,
Sandbox equals FART smarts.

If, then.
If, then.
If, then.

▫ ▫ ▫ ▫

But, Ms. J.

Wouldn't this plan be a
divergent
way to learn?

For us.
And for you.

The tree rustles.
Everyone holds their breath.
Time stops for a second.

Divergent, huh?

Ms. J's face
all-the-way
uncrinkles.

And she looks like Janie again,
savoring an organic s'mores
    Pop-Tart,

her small sideways smile
slowly slips across her face,
turning into a bigger
    sideways smile,
like she knows better,
but can't help it.

▫ ▫ ▫ ▫

I pick the book,
she says,
squishing her lips into a point.

I nod.

First ten minutes of class,
everyone takes turns
reading—
OUT LOUD,
she says,
staring us down.

We nod.

Everyone,
she says,
pointing at Javier,
who looked away
when Ms. J sa͙
out loud
and ͙ ͙asn't looked back.
͙t it?
I pick the book.
And if you take turns reading,
for ten solid minutes,
out loud,
then and only then,
we'll play your game,
for the last ten minutes
of class.

If you don't read,
you don't play.

We all nod.
Including Ms. J.

It looks like we have a
        deal, then,
she says.

The wind picks up speed,
whistling through the willow,
and even Jordan J's low
        fart noise
seems solemn in its own way.

BEN Y

<0benwhY>

aurs
ins.
n,
rain.

in just
am
their

d a butt brain.

ir back
?
rom other dinos?
eir tails work?
er tails do?

They
could
not
work
without the very important
very special
very weird
butt brain.

Dino butt brain
equals
knowing when to run
equals
knowing when to hide
equals
protection.

Fun fact:
I'm pretty sure I have two
        brains, too.
Regular brain.
Dino butt brain.

Sometimes
(a lot of times)
my regular brain

goes blank,
stalls,
can't reach any thought
or explanation,
so my dino butt brain kicks in

Shazam!

Sometimes it aims me
toward trouble
instead of away from it,
but maybe that's because
it knows the real trouble
is in my real brain
and that's what I need to
run away
from.

□ □ □ □

Benita?
Did you need something?

My real brain kicks in,
as I realize my dino brain
made me stay back
after class,
after Ms. J has made everyone

give her high fives and byes,
as the echoes of the day
fade into distant shouts
outside
and inside feels quiet,
nice.

Um.
It's Ben Y
not Benita.

My dino butt brain
parked me here.
In front of her desk
that is a table
and not an actual desk,
and it didn't tell me
why.

I wanted to tell you,
uh . . .

I love this quiet,
when everyone is gone,
when I can hide
after school
and breathe deep
for the first time

all day.
But usually,
when I stay
after school
in the cool
quiet
I'm by myself,
not standing here,
in front of an adult,
like a big ol' dork.

I wanted to tell you . . .
I'm sorry.
About the book.
I do things
sometimes
without thinking.
I say things
all of the time
without thinking.
And it's weird?
Because I'm always thinking
about something.
But then
the thing that happens
or the thing I say
isn't any of the things

I was thinking.
I might have a dino brain?
You know, near my butt?
Does that make any sense?

Anyway.

Sorry I made you so mad.

□ □ □ □

Her elbow on her desk,
her palm covering her mouth,
she looks up
through her long lashes
at me

and breathes,
making the same
sniffffffff noise
my baby sister, Esme, makes
after she cries
too

too

too

hard.

Benita.

Her voice twists,
making a spiral in the air,
flying above my head,
then diving
into my ear.

I really hate that name.
My name is Ben now.
Benita was buried in ashes
almost a year ago.
Gone.
Dust.
And Ben was born.
I don't have the
     mahogany voice,
and I know I'm not him,
but I can be my own Ben.
I am my own Ben.
I am enough Ben for both
     me and him.
And I want Ms. J to get it right.
Why can't she get it right?

Benita.
You need to understand—

Ms. J looks up.
The bottom of the stairs
slant over her too-small desk;
if she stood up fast,
whack,
she'd get a concussion.

She shakes her head.
She opens her mouth.
She closes it.
She opens it again.

What you did was wrong.
But also . . .
I'm sorry I got so mad.
It wasn't professional.

Ms. J does a ridiculous
     thing now,
sticking one bent elbow out
     to the side,
and sticking her other arm
straight out to the other side.
She nods her head into
     her elbow crook,
loud-whispers,
I lost my cool,

but don't worry,
I just found it again,
then winks at me,
while her head
is still
dabbed into
her elbow crook
and no,
omg,
just stop.

My dino butt brain
makes me laugh
so hard
because
oh wow,
she is such a weirdo goof,
not like any teacher I've
     ever known,
what is even happening.

▫ ▫ ▫ ▫

Ms. J stands now,
arms back down,
tilts her head
to the side,

slides
away from her desk
not smashing her head
on the stairs.

Shouldn't you be running
    for the bus?
How are you getting home?

I tilt my head
to the opposite side,
even though
I'm not
in danger
of smashing it.

Maybe I'm making fun of her?
Maybe I'm not?

I take the city bus.
I'm good.

Ms. J smiles.
Her eyebrows point down,
a little like the Grinch.
Well, then.
You have time.
Come with me for a minute?

Her question,
it's a command.
I don't say yes or no.
I just follow her
out of the stairwell,
her breeze
smelling like the tired perfume
that lives in a cloud
around every grown woman
I know.

▫ ▫ ▫ ▫

You may never have heard of
     a place such as this, but—

Ms. J's arms swing wide.
She tries to wink slowly
as she sing-talks,
but both eyes wink
at the same time
and I have to chew my cheek
to stop the sneak
of a laugh
from squeaking
out.

What if she thinks
that sneak laugh
is *with* her
and not
because of her?

It is definitely
because of her.

This
     is
               a
                    library.
This,
     Benita,
          is
               where
                    the books
                         live.

She continues to not get
my name right.
Sigh.

Her arms are still wide,
she's spreading her wings,
her caftan billowing,
like she has

her
own
personal
fan,
like
she is
Beyoncé
or
something.

Her voice gets
even louder now,
like she's singing
on a freaking
stage:

Please
    show
       me
           the
                tomes
that
    don't
      belong
        in a toilet.

Please
    help
      me
        choose
          a book
            for the class.

▫ ▫ ▫ ▫

Oh, man.

▫ ▫ ▫ ▫

On the first day of school
we had to play
Two Truths and a Lie
to get to know each other.

I said:

I have eleven toes.
I have two sisters.
I finish every book I read.

Was eleven toes my lie?
Or the reading thing?
They all argued,

but finally agreed,
it had to be the toes,
except
Jordan J
who ran around me
leaping
like a bonkers bananas deer
yelling
No one in here reads books!
No one in here finishes
    anything!
Take off your socks!

Ms. J told him to bring it down
six hundred notches
and then she moved along,
ready for the next
truths and lies
and lies and truths

but Jordan J was right.
I've never
ever
actually
by myself
ever

finished
reading
a book.
Any book.
Not one book.
In my whole life.
I've had books read to me.
Sometimes.
But I don't actually read them
on my own
ever.

In actual fact,
I have not actually
ever
been into this actual library
except once
for a FART study review
last year.

I swallow.

I look around.
The stacks and stacks of books
remind me swiftly,
fiercely,

of *his* room
filled with his own stacks
    of books,
his mahogany voice
drifting down the hall
as he read out loud
anything and everything
he could.

I don't think I can do this.
I don't think I can be in here.
I'm never going to read a book,
ever ever ever,
and I'm never coming in here
ever ever ever
again.

▫ ▫ ▫ ▫

*Whoa, we are far from
    done here.*
Where are you going?

Ms. J gently touches my elbow,
stopping me
before I can run.

Her hand is warm,
steady,
and for one weird second,
I almost put my hand
on top of her hand
to see if some of that
warm steadiness
might rub off on me.

I swallow the puffs of breath
shooting from my mouth,
choking them down
before they make me so dizzy
I have to sit right here
on the floor.

Hey.
It's okay.

She's looking at me hard now,
trying to find answers
to the whys I'm creating.

Just choose something
everyone will like.

I let the brightness of her stare
hold my gaze,
fill my eyes.
I don't blink
just in case
her laser stare
can outshine
my dark memories.

□ □ □ □

Not as easy as it seems, huh?

She's still looking at me
like I glitched
and grew two heads
for a second.

My one actual head
wakes up,
says to me:
*She's talking about choosing
    a book,*
dummy.

And, yeah,
there are
a million
a jillion
a brazillian
books in here.
Benicio would have loved
every
single
one.

I breathe.
I breathe.

Over there,
a red-and-white spine
winks
in the light.

I pick it up.

My stomach flutters
as I look over the cover.
It's like a whisper,
a little gift, maybe

from my brother
who can't technically
give gifts anymore.

What about this one?

I hold it up,
wave it at her
as a smile
squirms its way
to my face, and
little surprise
giggle bubbles
rise up
up
up
out of the darkness
that was just sinking me
a minute ago.

Ms. J's face
smushes into
a shriveled-up
pucker,
looking more like a

sourpuss starfish
than anything bright and shiny.

That?
That's not a book.

What!
Yes it is!

I wave it around.
It's so beat-up,
the cover almost falls off.

It has all these pages.
And an author.
And there's words in it.
Everything a book needs!
Plus, look . . .

I point to the shelf.
There are lots and lots
    of copies,
Because duh,
this is the kind of book
kids actually like.

Benita.
No.
Pick a real book.

This is a real book!
Everyone will love it.

Benicio would have loved
    it, too.
He might have even
just now
showed it to me
if you believe in that kind
    of thing.
(I don't say any of that out
    loud.)

Let me see it.

Her words come out all
    together,
in a long sigh,
like maybe
I just
poked a hole
in her belly
and all her hopes
and dreams

for me
are leaking
out
pshhhhhhhhhhhhhh
all
at
once.

She shakes her head,
but
she says:

Fine.

I nod my head
to show her
her head was doing it wrong.

Fine?

Fine.
But everyone better read.
Out loud.
Or I will choose another book.
A real one.
And that will be that.

□ □ □ □

SAVE UR SERVER SAVE UR SELF

A Many Choices Sandbox Adventure Book

by Tennessee Williamson

▫ ▫ ▫ ▫

It'll be great,
I say.
And the surprise giggle bubbles
squeak-pop around my words.
It might even have a horse in it.
AND a mouse.

Ms. J stops leaking
all her hopes
and dreams
for me
out of her mouth
in big long sighs
as she laughs
hard
before tossing
a fist bump
my way
and saying,

Girl.
Touché.

JORDAN J

<JordanJmageddon!!!!>

Ben Y has eleven toes. What?? I know!! Everyone else thinks that was her lie on the first day of class, because she said that was her lie, but I know the truth and not because I see her on the city bus every day and sometimes we even sit next to each other and talk about stuff like building a sky ship in Sandbox and how many fairies you would need to make it fly. I haven't ever seen her toes on the bus, but I still know her toes were not her lie. How? Because she said the thing about finishing every book she reads and her mouth did this thing where half of it turned down just a teeny tiny bit like when my sister Carolina says she ate her Brussels sprouts but I watch her feed them to Spartacus who immediately barfs them out on the floor because Spartacus is no dummy and Brussels sprouts are not the best, not because Spartacus is barfing all of her food these days. Also, I ALSO have never read a book to the end, either, and I feel like Ben Y and I are kind of in a secret club with each other that is so super secret that a) no one knows about it, including Ben Y, and b) we can't talk about it or else people will know that I also have never finished reading a book even though I'm twelve years old.

□ □ □ □

We really really really can't tell Ms. J (no relation) about this unfinished book situation because she went to library school and used to be a librarian and then decided to teach in a classroom instead of a library or at least that's what she told us when we all thought being a librarian was her lie but really her lie was she owns three pairs of jeans. She actually owns zero pairs of jeans which is even more

shocking than having been a librarian which I guess isn't that shocking if you think about how much she loves books and wants us to
love books all the books forever books books books books big books
little books boooooooooooooooorks.

□ □ □ □

So I don't know about this reading out loud in class situation. It feels
dicey on like seventeen different levels because, one: reading out loud
is worse than reading and nothing is worse than reading. Two: reading
can never be as interesting as making an amusement park in Sandbox
where trampolines are made of sheep and every time you jump on a
sheep you make it poo and the poo falls in a lava pit and catches on
fire and the smoke fills a hot-air balloon and you ride in the hot-air
balloon to the platform in the sky where you can jump off and land
back on the sheep trampoline to start over again, or you can swim in
the platform pool that is filled with baked beans because baked beans
are my favorite.

□ □ □ □

What was I talking about again? Oh! Right! This book. The thing is,
though, when Ms. J was all, *Benita, can you come in front of the class
please, and make a very special announcement?* and Ben Y was all,
My name is Ben Y not Benita, Here's the new book, and her face did
this sideways cat-smile thing like she knew something we didn't know,

I got super confused because she seemed almost happy about the book and then she showed us the book and I was even more confused because is that even a real book?

□ □ □ □

It said *Save Ur Server, Save Ur Self* on the cover in the Sandbox font and Ms. J's face scrunched up like she had eaten really old baked beans people had been swimming in and Ben B and Javier and me all looked at each other and Ben Y winked really big like a grandma who slips you a candy bar after your mom lets all the breath out of her mouth and says, *No more candy, Mother, please.*

□ □ □ □

Wait, so it's a book about Sandbox and cool, cool, does that count as a real book? Ms. J said no and Ben Y said yes both at the same time and everyone laughed and then Ms. J read the first part out loud to show us how she wants us to do it and she used silly voices and kind of danced around and it made me want to dig a hole in the ground so she could fall into it and be saved from her own self because, holy cats, she was so embarrassing, and THEN she made Ben Y start reading out loud for two minutes and thirty seconds in a row which doesn't sound like a long time but is actually about twenty years and a million seconds long when you're reading out loud, a thing I know now that I had to go second after Ben Y.

□ □ □ □

Javier shook his head and wouldn't open his mouth when it was his turn and Ms. J blew snorts of air out of her nose like how a gnu would, or no, not a gnu but one of those other big animals that get mad and breathe hard. Warthog? No. Ms. J is prettier than a warthog. Probably prettier than a gnu, too, but I don't know what a gnu looks like and also I like to say gnu gnu gnu in my head over and over and now Javier had to move his desk next to Ms. J's desk and he's facing the rest of us, even though he's looking at his notebook and not at us and everyone else had already had a turn reading so we had to skip Javier and start over and Ben Y had to read for ANOTHER two minutes and thirty seconds or else we wouldn't have a total of ten minutes and wouldn't be able to play Sandbox and Ben Y snorted like a gnu, too and Javier better watch out because Ben Y is going to trample him she's so mad.

□ □ □ □

I guess it's time to hold up my end of the bargain. Those were the words Ms. J said when she scooched a chair up to the computer in the corner that no one ever uses. Ben B helped her get it all turned on and then there it was! Sandbox in school which was super weird like seeing a tiger at the dentist's office and then we all realized something at the same time . . . Ms. J has never played! Which duh, but also it's been so long since any of us was a noob we forgot about SETUP. A name, an avatar, choosing strengths, choosing weaknesses, playing on the noob servers until you have enough gold to level up to real servers, it's like A LOT. And ALL of us forgot she was going to have to do all of that and none of that is fun to watch and it's going to take a hundred years if we can only do ten minutes at a time and aaaaaaargh. It would almost be better if she WERE a teacher griefer because then at least we'd be PLAYING.

□ □ □ □

[Fart noise]

□ □ □ □

According to my mom, happy accidents are the next best thing to small miracles, which is an interesting thing to think about especially right now while I'm wondering if it will be a small miracle or a happy accident if Ms. J EVER gets out of setup, omgggggggggg and so Ben B is going to create a server with a password that's just for all of us in class so we can meet tonight and chat about what to do to make this happy accident or small miracle happen faster because omgggggggggg we are all going to die, just wither up into skeletons with beards while we wait for Ms. J to decide if she wants *blue hair or pink hair or no hair or maybe she should be a dragon why are there so many choices how did you all choose?* Seriously seriously this is why grownups should not play video games. Or maybe it's actually why they don't play video games? Ooh. Deep thought. Anyway, it is setup 911 over here.

JAVIER

<JaJaJavier:)>

THINGS JAVIER WILL NEVER DO IN CLASS

33) SURVIVE ALL SUMMER

1) READ OUT LOUD
2) read out loud
3) READ OUT LOUD
4) read out loud
5) r e a d   o u t   l o u d
6) READ OUT LOUD
7) read out loud
8) (read out loud)
9) read out loud
10) READ OUT LOUD
11) read out loud
12) READ OUT LOUD
13) Read Out loud
14) READ OUT LOUD
15) read out loud
16) read out loud
17) READ OUT LOUD
18) read out loud
19) READ OUT LOUD
20) read out loud
21) READ OUT LOUD
22) read out loud
23) READ OUT LOUD
24) read OUT LOUD
25) read out loud
26) READ out loud
27) READ OUT LOUD
28) read out loud
29) READ OUT LOUD
30) Read out loud
31) Play Sandbox
32) MAKE FRIENDS

69

 CHAT

Divergent Dingleberries

Private server created by: **BenBee**

Password required

Avatar name:

Password:

Remember! Ghost Season is coming! Protect your lives, your health, and your gold by avoiding ghosts at all costs. Think you can outsmart the ghosts by logging out? Think again! All logged out avatars will remain in sleeping mode, so make sure you're protected. Get melted during Ghost Season? Gonna cost ya!

In order to bring you the very best game possible, Sandbox is moving to a pay-per-play model. Survive Ghost season? You'll maintain VIP status and continue on the free platform. Get melted? You can retrieve your gold and items when you sign up for one of our affordable monthly plans. Click here for more details.

0benwhY?! ENTERS GAME

0benwhY: benbee my dude
0benwhY: divergent dingleberries, rly?

BenBee: what. dingleberry pie is delicious.

0BenwhY: omg, ben b, that's huckleberry. or blackberry. or mulberry.
0BenwhY: literally ANY other berry

jajajavier:) ENTERS GAME

jajajavier:): hey nerds, i mean dingleberries

0BenY?!: HE SPEAKS!!

BenBee: Javier, hey, u found the server.

jajajavier:): of course i did. i'm not Ms. J.

0BenwhY: Har har.
0benwhY: Dude, seriously, tho
0benwhY: you threw me under the reading bus today
0benwhY: super extra ugly nasty not cool at all i want to strangle u what were u thinking

jajajavier:): sorry

jajajavier:): soooo we need to get ms. J out of setup, huh?

jajajavier:): y don't we just give her homework

jajajavier:): she can finish setup at home on her own

ObenwhY: y do u even care, Javier?

ObenwhY: if u wont read u cant play so . . .

jajajavier:): not reading doesn't mean i don't care

jajajavier:): cause im never gonna read out loud. zero percent chance of that.

jajajavier:): but its boring to listen to Ms. J spend 56538562 hours in setup

BenBee: but you nodded. under the tree. when she made us promise. to read.

jajajavier:): i nodded bc if i didn't, she would've said no. i nodded to help u help her help u.

BenBee: but if u don't read you'll never get to play.

jajajavier:): ill survive

ObenwhY: oh nuh uh u will not survive bc I will make u eat the book if u do that to me again

ObenwhY: and u will have to go to the hospital

ObenwhY: for emergency book removal surgery

ObenwhY: and then I will strangle u

ObenwhY: and then u wont be able to give any more advice

jajajavier:): I'm really sorry, ok. Really.

jajajavier:): but come on, we all know its gonna take 57254735 years to get ms j out of setup

ObenwhY: ugh, I knowwwwwww, and i hate that ur right

BenBee: maybe she doesn't need her own avatar.

BenBee: maybe she can just play as one of us.

ObenwhY: RU bonkers?????

ObenwhY: ms j? playing as me? HAHAHA.

ObenwhY: that's not the kind of divergent thinking we need, mr. dingleberry

jajajavier:): no way shes playing as me

jajajavier:): noobs get melted like 4629562895 times

jajajavier:): i'd lose all my gold

BenBee: ok fine, good point, no way i can lose all my gold.

BenBee: this homework idea, hmm.

BenBee: it isn't terrible, even if no one likes jajajavier right now.

jajajavier:): hey! I'm a likeable guy! 😊 ❤️ 🎩

jajajavier:): u just have to get to know me

0benwhY: but u don't talk

jajajavier:): im talking write now. with my hands. hello, nice to chat with u Ben Y

jajajavier:): what r ur hobbies besides yelling at new kids?

jajajavier:): what r yr favorite snacks besides the souls of ppl who wrong u?

0benwhY: 💀 🔪 😒

BenBee: 😄 i like to play Sandbox and eat cheesy puffs.

jajajavier:): same!

0benwhY: hey! focus! wont she, like, give us homework if we give her homework?

BenBee: she already gives us homework.

0benwhY: ah, yes, good point. i forgot bc i never do it

BenBee: maybe one of us can just use her login.

BenBee: finish her setup without her.

ObenwhY: no! benbee! your avatar is you. she has to be her.

ObenwhY: we can't make her her

ObenwhY: only she can do that

BenBee: fine.

BenBee: looks like its homework then.

jajajavier:): BOOM. who has two thumbs and is a smart dude?

JORDANJMAGEDDON!!!! ENTERS GAME

JORDANJMAGEDDON!!!!: Ben Y?

ObenwhY: omg, shut up, Jordan. i am not a dude.

JORDANJMAGEDDON!!!!: 😄

ObenwhY: i can be a girl with short hair, dingleberry, even with a new name

jajajavier:): dude, misgendering people to make a joke isn't ok. im an idiot & even i know that

ObenwhY: thanks. and don't kiss up to me. im still mad at u.

JORDANJMAGEDDON!!!!:

ObenwhY: im mad at u too

BenBee: can everyone zip it?
BenBee: did you see the thing about Ghost Season?
BenBee: maybe we should do something to protect our avatars.
BenBee: for when Ghost season gets here.

BenBee: we have this cool server all to ourselves.
BenBee: we could make a pyramid out of diamonds so we can hide there.
BenBee: ghosts. coming. melting. everyone.
BenBee: devs r cleaning house, archiving avatars that get melted during ghost season.
BenBee: u'll have to pay real actual money to get unarchived.
BenBee: we need the pyramid to survive. well, to keep playing for free.
BenBee: and i know for sure my parents won't pay a monthly fee so i can play sandbox.
BenBee: no way, no how.
BenBee: guys, come on! is anyone gonna give U money so u can play?

ObenwhY: don't call us guys.

jajajavier:): ugh I gotta jet. ill help with the pyramid 2morow after school
jajajavier:): I've been been hiding in the bathroom with the laptop
jajajavier:): my mom thinks im pooping myself to death

jajajavier:) HAS EXITED GAME

BenBee: dang dang dang moms coming up the stairs.
BenBee: im supposed to b practicing handwriting, barf.
BenBee: shes gonna kill me.
BenBee: i gotta jet 2.

BenBee HAS EXITED GAME

ObenwhY: looks like its up to us to get this pyramid started

JORDANJMAGEDDON!!!!: 🖐 🖐

ObenwhY: im still sort of mad at u, but not as mad at u as i am Javier, so fine
ObenwhY: 🖐 🖐

JORDANJMAGEDDON!!!!: 😍

ObenwhY: okay okay don't get too excited.

JORDANJMAGEDDON!!!!:

ObenwhY: r u gonna haul those diamonds over
here or what?
ObenwhY: also, whos gonna be the one to ask ms j?
ObenwhY: about the setup homework?

JORDANJMAGEDDON!!!!:

ObenwhY: mmm hmm great of course

JORDANJMAGEDDON!!!!:

ObenwhY: glad to see ur finally into building this thing
cause i gotta go. dinner time.

ObenwhY EXITS GAME

JORDANJMAGEDDON!!!!: ?

JORDANJMAGEDDON!!!!:

BEN B

<BenBee>

You've done thirty minutes?
Of handwriting practice?
To earn your fifteen minutes
of Sandbox?

Mom leaned around my
    doorway
just as I clicked off the
    monitor.

Uh, I reversed it.
Fifteen minutes of Sandbox,
then handwriting, here I come.

I held up a pencil,
tried to smile.

Dad curled around Mom,
filling up
my whole
bedroom doorway.

That's not how it works, pal.
You can't take advantage of
    your mom that way.
No screens.
One week.

What!
Dad!
Mom and I had a deal!
And I was just about to—

Jim . . .
Mom twisted her face up to
    look at him.
I don't th—

Keep talking to me like that,
    Benjamin,
Dad interrupted Mom,
and you'll make it two weeks
no screens.

But Dad!
I was just about to start!
Mom said—

Benjamin.
What did I say?
Don't use that tone with me.
Now it's two weeks.

DAD!

Three *weeks!*
Want to make it more?

I hate how Dad doesn't yell.
I hate how the angrier he gets,
the calmer he acts.

Mom pushed her way
away from Dad,
stomped off,
leaving me
with three weeks
no screens.

Dad ran his hand
through his hair,
down his face,
said,

I bet,
in three weeks,
your handwriting will be better
than mine.

Then he pointed finger
    guns at me,
smiled,
walked away.

Come on, Jenny,
his voice drifted into my room,
from down the hall.
Come out of the bathroom.
You're too easy on him.

That's when I put in my
earbuds,
shut
my
door
and
here I am.

▫ ▫ ▫ ▫

No screens.
Three weeks.

Three weeks!

Now there's nothing fun
waiting for me
at the end of my days
of nothing fun.

I am a boring snake
eating my own boring tail.

Three weeks.
Might as well be
three forevers.

□ □ □ □

At least there's Sandbox
　　at school.

□ □ □ □

But not really.
Not like I thought it would be.
Ms. J gets to play
on that one rickety
old computer,
that one
beard-growing
old man of a machine
while we watch her
finally decide
after a hundred and fifty years
she wants purple hair
for her avatar
with no gold.

We need more machines,
so she can watch us and learn,
so we can all teach her
together.

That's how it has to work,
that's how she'll figure it out.
Computers for everyone.
It only makes sense.
Just like a book for each of us.
It's the best way.
The only way.
Shazam.

And I'll get to play.
Every day.
Take THAT, no screens
for three weeks.

□ □ □ □

More computers?

Ms. J shakes her head.

Tall order, Ben B.
An impossible feat.

But . . .
My voice sputters as my
    brain spins,
no way she can say no
    that easily,
no way this question is already
    answered.

But . . .
I hear my voice winding up,
louder, with a begging edge.
We each have a book to read—
we should also each
have a machine.
Right?
So we can teach you better.
You know?

Ms. J shakes her head.

Books are curriculum, Ben B.
And I'm not even sure this—
she flings her hand back
    and forth
like she's waving away a stink—
even counts as a book.

Ben Y yells, *HEY!*
Ms. J ignores her.

Computer allotments aren't
the same as books.
Requisitions, paperwork,
grants . . .
it's a process.

Three weeks, no screens.
Three weeks, no screens.
It's burned into my brain,
the only thing
on repeat.

So it's just No?
That's it?
You can't even try?

I'm arguing with a teacher,
my voice a whine
even I don't like,
pushing my luck, I know,
but three weeks no screens.
Three weeks no screens!

We're trying so hard.
Every day.
Reading out loud.
Summer school.
The FART retake looming,
a shadow over
every day
and yet here we are
doing this thing we hate
so we can teach you to love
a new thing.
Come on. . . .
Can't you meet us halfway?

Halfway!
Ben B!
What do you call this?
She waves the book at me.
This isn't literature.
It barely has sentence
      structure.
This is floof,
fun.
You all need an extra life
when it comes to the
assessment retake,
and this isn't that!

But I press on,
making magic out of nonsense,
trying to cobble together
      extra lives
for all of you.
This is so much further
than halfway.

Farther! Ben Y shouts.
Ms. J ignores her.

All kinds of feelings boil up
      from my belly,
strong and steaming.

So when you said
Help me help you,
I guess I should have known.
No deal with a grown-up is
      a real deal, ever.
Is that what a divergent
      plan is?
Just a trick.
A stupid trick.
You were never going to play,
      were you?
Not for real.

You never cared about helping
us help you, did you?

The words zip from my mouth,
darts toward a fluttering target,
finding a bull's-eye
as Ms. J sucks in her breath
and for a tiny split-second
looks away
before she looks back,
with sparks in her eyes
and fire in her voice
as she says,

Enough.
ENOUGH.

▫ ▫ ▫ ▫

And now we read out loud
so this day can win a prize
for being the worst day

in the history
of ever.

▫ ▫ ▫ ▫

Javier shakes his head
no,
holds his palm
on his closed book,
like he's swearing the truth
and only the truth
that he will never read out loud
in class,
so help him,
Flying Spaghetti Monster.

One more chance, Javier.
This is it.
Don't test me.
I am already
in
a
mood.

But it's a test he takes anyway,
still refusing to read,
until Ms. J, possibly about to
turn into a fire-breathing
    dragon
(which is also probably
mostly
my fault)

makes him move his desk
next to hers
so he has to face all of us
while he doesn't read.

Someone will have to read
twice now.
If we want to hit our ten
     minutes.
If we want any Sandbox today.
Even if it's stupid setup.
And it'll be my only
     Sandbox, too.
No screens three weeks,
still on repeat,
banging around in my head.

I hate this day.

▫ ▫ ▫ ▫

Two minutes and thirty
seconds
plus
two minutes and thirty seconds
equals

way too many minutes and
     seconds.
That's just
simple math.

Unseen dangers lie
ahead, do you build
a fortress to protect
your village?
Go to page 15.

Or do you forge ahead?
Go to page 20.

I look up.
My mouth is dry.
Am in a desert?
These unmoving boulders
of letters and sounds and
     words,
tripping me until I move
     so slow,
I must be on the verge of . . .
I am going to die of . . .
word poisoning?

As the reader of the moment,
it's your choice, Ben B.

To die?
I ask.

Her expression has not
changed
from earlier today,
when my words
were sharp
and she was soft.

No, Ben B.
Her voice hard and flat.
Fortress or forge ahead?

I look at Javier,
who doesn't seem to care:
he's being forced to face us
as he doesn't read.
He's not even looking at me,
because he's drawing,
always drawing.
What could he possibly
    be drawing
so much of,
all the time?

The grouchiness pushes
    through,
words flying from my mouth
that I couldn't catch
even if I wanted to.

These choices are stupid.
Everyone knows you catch
    a fairy,
squish it,
use the dust to fly,
survey your surroundings
    from above,
THEN decide what to do.
You can see everything
while you're safe in the air.
Duh!
What dummy wrote this thing?

Quietly, a voice behind me says:
My mom did. My mom wrote
it. She's a great writer. The best.
Why are you saying mean
things about my mom, the
smartest mom in the actual
whole world?

Everyone's head jerks up.
Even Javier's.
Ben Y clasps her hands to
    her mouth.
The color drains from
    Ms. J's face.

Then Jordan J busts out
    laughing.
*Just kidding. My mom works
at a newspaper. She's just a
regular mom.*

I spin in my seat so fast,
an angry gyroscope.
*Shut up, Jordan.
This isn't a joke.
Some stupid person wrote this
    stupid book
and now we have to read it—
some of us have to read
    EXTRA—
and Ms. J can't even play,
like she promised.*

Aaaaargh.

*Let's forge ahead, stupidly,
to see what stupid choice
we have next.*

▫ ▫ ▫ ▫

So, yeah.
Now I'm sitting in the hallway.
While I think about
how to think about
my words
before
I say them
and the choices I make,
which,
agreed,
have been pretty stupid
today.

▫ ▫ ▫ ▫

I think about:
extra weeks of no screens
if Ms. J calls my parents.

I think about:
that would be guts-meltingly
    terrible.

I think about:
what Dad would say about my
        tone today,
about my attitude today.

I think about:
if I say I'm sorry,
then Ms. J will not call
        my parents.

▫ ▫ ▫ ▫

Sorry, Ms. J.
Yes, I have cooled off.
Yes, I know stupid *is not a*
divergent use of vocabulary.
Yes, I know you're doing the
        best you can.
Yes, I know we all are.

▫ ▫ ▫ ▫

I still hate this day.

▫ ▫ ▫ ▫

Ben Y reads out loud now.
She spits every word,
like she's angry at it,
for ever being in her mouth
to begin with.

I don't know what she's mad
        about,
but right on.

She finishes her part,
looks up from her book,
catches me looking at her.

Thumbs up, Ben Y,
I like how you spit your words.

She doesn't look at me.
I don't know where she's
        looking.
Maybe she's imagining this
        day is over.
I'm going to imagine that, too.

BEN Y

<0benwhY>

I don't like to rush.
I don't like to hurry.
I don't like to be home on time.
I don't like to be home at all.

So I stay places.
As long as I can.
At school.
On the bus.
Wherever.

I'm
an
easy
sneak,

a shadow
bending
into quiet places.

Like today,
this old space,
storage
behind the gym,
full of boxes,

junk,
broken stuff . . .
now I'm part of its mess, too.

It's quiet in here,
the wifi works,
I can surf
fashion blogs,
imagine
lines of clothes
I might design
one day
in another world
another place
far freaking away
from here.

And when the light
goes from fluorescent
to mauve
I know
it's time to pack up.
Vacate.
Head home.

I can take the city bus.
Sneak into my room.
Move past the memories,
dark in their own shadows.

Except.
Today, I hear a rustle.
Today, I'm not alone.

There's another sneak.
Uh-oh.

▫ ▫ ▫ ▫

Ms. J.
She stands in the shadows,
a pushcart full of old
computers
in front of her
and a look on her face
that says
O Ben Why
and
O Ben How
and
O Ben I Wish You Weren't
    Here Right Now.

▫ ▫ ▫ ▫

I can feel it.
The why inside me,
wiggling
shivering
to get out.

It moves
up my throat.
Bounces
on my tongue.
Hits up
against my teeth.
Pushing.
Shoving.
Trying to break free
until it's too strong,
I'm too weak,
and out it flies,
making us both jump,

Why
are
you
here?

What
are
you
doing?

Ms. J stays
frozen.
My mouth stays
a little bit open.

Then my restless whys
break through
her ice:

Benita.
Well.
As long as you're here,
I could use your help.

□ □ □ □

Not Benita.
Ben Y.

□ □ □ □

I look down at the pushcart.
I look up at her.

She looks down at the
    pushcart.
She looks up at me.

It's . . .
It's a long story.
And our class needs
    computers.
Even though Ben B was
quite
quite
rude,
I do think he was right.

I nod.

She keeps talking,
explaining herself,
like I'm the police
or like I could get her in
    trouble
or something.

Trying to requisition
computers,
it takes forever.
Really. It's like pulling teeth.

My lips suck against my teeth,
protecting them.

These are just sitting here.
No one will miss them.

I hitch my backpack
over my shoulder,
wait for her to realize
I'm the one who should be
    in trouble.
I'm the one trespassing
after school.

She's watching me.
I can almost see the gears
moving
behind her eyes,
then:

How about, if you help me get
these to our classroom,
I won't ask you why you're
here so late.
Cool?

I nod.
Cool.

My *cool* sounds like a question,
too.

    ▫ ▫ ▫ ▫

We didn't just steal those
computers, right?
Teachers don't steal, right?

JORDAN J

`<JordanJmageddon!!!!>`

I think maybe I just saw Ben Y and Ms. J (no relation) stealing a whole bunch of computers.

□ □ □ □

It sounds really weird to think that out loud, so probably I'm wrong, except I definitely saw them pushing a cart loaded with computers around the outside of the building toward the door that opens into the back of the stairwell.

□ □ □ □

Why would they be moving around a bunch of computers outside when they could just walk down any hallway inside school and not worry about one of the computers falling off the cart and landing in a splotch of mud which is exactly what just happened?

□ □ □ □

I mean, unless they were stealing them.

□ □ □ □

I am like at least eighty-seven percent sure teachers don't steal things, but I am also maybe only forty-seven percent sure Ben Y doesn't steal things, so the math here is weird and confusing like a FART test word question I have to read sixty-five times before it still doesn't make sense and I just move to the next question.

□ □ □ □

The window in the door that opens into the back of the stairwell is super dusty dirty so it's hard to see inside, but I'm peeking anyway. I'm good at peeking in dusty windows, not because I'm a creeper, I'm definitely not a creeper, but because I like to go to the back of the gym and look through the dusty windows on the gym doors so I can watch the dance team.

▫ ▫ ▫ ▫

Wait.

▫ ▫ ▫ ▫

That DOES make me sound like a creeper. I'm not, though, I just watch them because the dances look pretty fun and I have some super sweet dance moves, too, though if I'm being honest here, my super sweet dance moves are about a hundred times better than theirs, it's just that there aren't any boys on the dance team and there's not, like, a boys' dance team, so I watch through the dusty windows and know in my heart that I could make the whole dance team go WHOA, JORDAN J DANG, SON, if I wanted to, which I kind of do, but also I kind of don't for some reasons and my mom always says to me: *Make smart choices, Jordan!* and so I peek through the windows until I make a smart choice.

▫ ▫ ▫ ▫

So yeah. I have experience looking in dusty windows.

▫ ▫ ▫ ▫

Ben Y and Ms. J have their backs turned to me and I can't really see anything else because the windows are small and it's getting dark outside so I should get going, but this was all very weird and interesting and it will definitely give me something to think about while Mom is yelling at me for coming home so late.

□ □ □ □

Oh! Hang on. I remember Ben B said something about everyone needing a computer to play Sandbox in class and duh, of course we do, but also duh where are we all going to find a computer? I guess Ben Y and Ms. J figured out the answer to that mystery question so hooray. Also hooray because that means those were definitely totally legit computers being pushcarted through mud puddles outside in the almost dark. One hundred percent legit.

□ □ □ □

Time for a one hundred percent legit dance move to celebrate me solving this mystery. *BOOYAH, Jordan J,* my brain says to myself, which is what Veronica Verve, famous judge of *Fierce Across America* the best dance competition TV show ever invented would say to me if she just saw me land that jeté and then drop into a baby freeze which is the thing I just did which was AWESOME and it's too bad Veronica Verve *didn't* see it in real life because she'd give me ten out of ten. Or maybe eight out of ten because baby freezes aren't very hard to do.

JAVIER

<JaJaJavier:)>

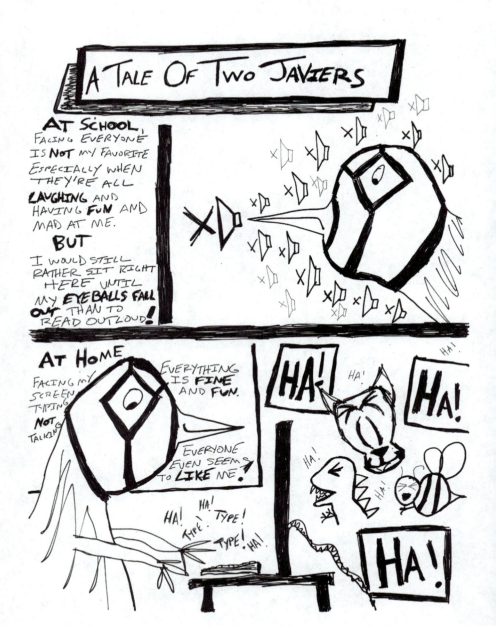

A Tale Of Two Javiers

AT SCHOOL, FACING EVERYONE IS **NOT** MY FAVORITE ESPECIALLY WHEN THEY'RE ALL **LAUGHING** AND HAVING **FUN** AND MAD AT ME.

BUT

I WOULD STILL RATHER SIT RIGHT HERE UNTIL MY **EYEBALLS FALL OUT** THAN TO READ OUTLOUD!

XD

AT HOME FACING MY SCREEN TYPING **NOT** TALKING

EVERYTHING IS **FINE** AND **FUN**.

EVERYONE EVEN SEEMS TO **LIKE** ME.

HA! TYPE! TYPE! TYPE! HA!

HA! HA! HA! HA! HA! HA!

100

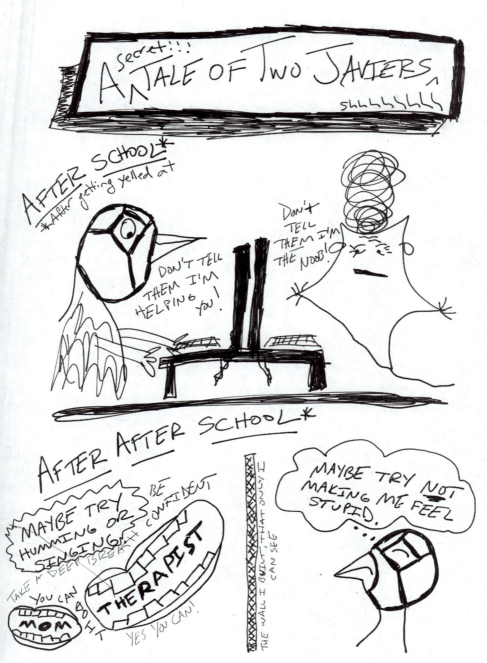

BEN B

<BenBee>

Wide eyes
meet wide eyes
as we gather under our stairs.
Our desks, pushed close,
making room for—

Read first.
Then we discuss . . .

those.

□ □ □ □

Benjamin Hobart Bellows.

Ms. J looks directly at me,
eyes sparking and arcing.

Ben Y. Javier. Jordan J
all snicker
as they mouth
Hobart?

You have zero lives left
in the game of summer school.
You used them all up
*   yesterday.*
Do you hear me?
Never speak to me

the way you spoke to me
*   yesterday*
ever
ever
again.
Got it?

Her earring hoops dangle,
shiver slightly,
are so thin, so wide,
I imagine them spinning,
flying from her ears,
lopping my head off.

I nod.
My hand touches my neck.

We all have a lot of feelings
*   sometimes,*
she says,
staring me down
until I shrink
in my seat.
But those feelings should
*   never be used*
to damage other people's
*   feelings.*
Do you hear me?

I nod.
I keep a careful eye on her
    dancing hoops.
I guess I never thought about
    teachers having feelings.
I guess that was pretty dumb.
I guess I get to keep my head
    today, despite being dumb.
Whew.

▫ ▫ ▫ ▫

Jordan J!
You read first.
Convince me your
    mother's words
are worthy
of being called a book.

She winks.
We laugh.

All of you.
Today is the day you
    convince me
I haven't made

a
huge
mistake.

▫ ▫ ▫ ▫

Hope leaps,
inside my guts
as I peek up
from my book,
counting the machines
pressed against the wall,
monitors dark,
wires coiled.

Yes.
Yes.
Yes.
Yes.
Yes.

The perfect amount.
She did it.
Enough computers for us all.

▫ ▫ ▫ ▫

You all read brilliantly today.
Except for Javier,
who also has used up every
extra life
and will be dealt with after I
 call his mother,
an experience neither he, nor I,
 nor his mother will enjoy,
I'm sure.
I will see you after class, Javier.

Javier doesn't look up
from his notebook,
just presses harder
and harder
with his pencil.

Ms. J spreads her arms
 wide now,
a ringmaster,
a car salesman on TV.

These are for the rest of you.

(Jordan J whistles
low and long.)

Ms. J's hands bend to her hips,
holding tight,
her head tilts,
meaning business.

However.
It's important you all
 know this—
Are you listening?
Jordan.
Get back in your seat.
Now is not the time for a
 baby freeze.

Everyone?

These computers are for
typing practice.

Her voice dips low,
a smile fights its way
to her face.

You will type
ALL communications to me
and to each other
during the ten minutes of

typing practice

at the end
of each class.

No speaking.
No noise.
No play.
Okay?

Repeat after me:
These computers are for

　　typing practice.

We repeat after her.

We are improving our sentence
　　structure skills.

We repeat after her.

We are practicing grammar
　　and spelling.

We repeat after her.

She nods.
Our chairs spring out
　　behind us
as we leap up,
but—
she holds out her hand.

Wait.
One more thing.

▫ ▫ ▫ ▫

It's like we're playing
　　freeze tag,
except we're all so excited,
we wiggle
while we stand,
not really frozen at all,
while we wait
for Ms. J's
one more thing.

At some point this summer,
our class will have a visitor.
Actually, I will have a visitor.
An administrator will
　　assess me,

my teaching ability,
my handling of the classroom.
Think of it like . . .
a FART for teachers.

Ha! She called it the FART!

I don't know when the
    assessment will be,
I don't know who will do it,
I just know it will happen.

So please, everyone,
remember:

typing practice.

And always be on your best
    behavior.

□ □ □ □

I want to ask
if this means she failed
the teacher FART,
just like we all failed
the FART FART,
and *that's* why
she's teaching
summer school.
But . . .
she drops her stop hand,
freeze tag is over,
and we all scramble
to the computers,
as fast as we can,
any questions erased
by the chimes and pings
of computers
coming
alive.

#

Divergent Dingleberries

Private server created by: **BenBee**

Password required

Avatar name:

Password:

Remember! Ghost Season is coming! Protect your lives, your health, and your gold by avoiding ghosts at all costs. Think you can outsmart the ghosts by logging out? Think again! All logged out avatars will remain in sleeping mode, so make sure you're protected. Get melted during Ghost Season? Gonna cost ya!

In order to bring you the very best game possible, Sandbox is moving to a pay-per-play model. Survive Ghost season? You'll maintain VIP status and continue on the free platform. Get melted? You can retrieve your gold and items when you sign up for one of our affordable monthly plans. Click here for more details.

JORDANJMAGEDDON!!!! ENTERS GAME
0BenwhY ENTERS GAME
BenBee ENTERS GAME

JORDANJMAGEDDON!!!!: 👩🏾➕j👉🏻👶🏻❄️❓❓❓

0BenwhY: JordanJMageddon ru asking Ms. J to do a baby freeze? what? why?

JORDANJMAGEDDON!!!!: 😂

BenBee: u guys don't make ms j regret getting these computers.

0BenwhY: pls don't say u guys, say everyone or yall or people or something that's not u guys
0BenwhY: kthx

BenBee: ty ty ty ty ty for the computers, ms j

0BenwhY: um do yall hear something?
0BenwhY: talking?
0BenwhY: hmm?

BenBee: i thought u said no talking, ms. j

JORDANJMAGEDDON!!!!: 🚫 💬

OBenwhY: huh! how does that not include u?

BenBee: ten times no fair, ms j. u can't just make rules and break rules!

BenBee: 2morrow when u play noooo talking.

BenBee: ok yes i know, limited time. so here's the plan for 2day, ms j.

BenBee: bc u have no avatar yet and bc setup is soooooo long u have 2 watch us.

BenBee: we'll show u some basics that u can practice on ur own once u have ur avatar.

JORDANJMAGEDDON!!!!!:

OBenwhY: 2nite, for ur homework, u finish ur setup, create ur avatar and practice a little, k?

OBenwhY: giving you homework was jajajavier:)'s idea, btw.

BenBee: then, if u finish ur homework 2nite, u get to join in the fun 2morrow, ms. j.

OBenwhY: ok. whos ready to learn? Did someone say Ms. J? Great!

OBenwhY: this is a pickax

BenBee: this is a diamond.

OBenwhY: Whatever! It totally looks like a diamond.

JORDANJMAGEDDON!!!!:

0BenwhY: we're building a pyramid
0BenwhY: yes out of diamonds

BenBee: so we can have a safe place 2 hide during Ghost Season.
BenBee: the ghosts will melt us and make us lose all our stuff.
BenBee: well this game is not suppose to be real life.

0BenwhY: and get archived
0BenwhY: and have to pay to get un-archived.
0BenwhY: so stupid

JORDANJMAGEDDON!!!!: 👻 x 10 😱

0BenwhY: no. nobody can kill ghosts
0BenwhY: except Ghostkiller

BenBee: Ghostkiller isn't real.

0BenwhY: wrong

BenBee: gamemakers created him to make people play more. A fake legend.

0BenwhY: UR SO wrong

BenBee: bogus.

BenBee: I mean, have u ever actually seen him OBenwhY?

OBenwhY: what does seeing ghostkiller prove? have u seen every player who ever played???

BenBee: that's what I thought.

JORDANJMAGEDDON!!!!: 😖 👉 😖

OBenwhY: yes, let's ignore BenBee for a minute. Ur in timeout!

OBenwhY: Ms. J, r u watching? u push this if u want to dig

BenBee: like this.

BenBee: ez.

BenBee: want 2 try it real quick w my avatar?

OBenwhY: Ahh! No! Ms. J! Stop! You're hitting ME with the pick ax. Hit the ground!

JORDANJMAGEDDON!!!!: 😂 😂 😂 😂 😂 😂

BenBee: ok ok lets not do that again.

OBenwhY: u push this to see where ur supplies are stored

JORDANJMAGEDDON!!!!: 🐵

BenBee: yeah. that's how we remember everything.

OBenwhY: what, r u surprised we all have brains???

BenBee: u'll remember 2.
BenBee: once u play for a while.

OBenwhY: Over there? that's our amusmetn park

BenBee: u can ride the pig swing 2morrow.

OBenwhY: but only if u do ur homework
OBenwhY: JordanJmageddon!!!! built the pig swing
OBenwhY: Cool, huh?

JORDANJMAGEDDON!!!!: 🐷 🎮 🎢 🎉

OBenwhY: uh, yeah, good luck getting him to use
words instead of emojis, Ms. J
OBenwhY: way to shoot for the sky

BenBee: Aw dang, hows it the bell already?
BenBee: ty again for the computers, Ms. j.
BenBee: im rly rly rly am sorry for being a turd
yesterday.
BenBee: im also sorry for saying turd just now.

0BenwhY: thanks for the computers 😜

0BenwhY: and don't foregt ur homework ms j

0BenwhY: cu 2morrow!

JORDANJMAGEDDON!!!!: 🙏

JORDANJMAGEDDON!!!! EXITS GAME

0BenwhY EXITS GAME

BenBee EXITS GAME

BEN B

<BenBee>

<cont.>

She never lets us leave
    class fast.
Most teachers do,
but not Ms. J.

We hop from foot to foot,
ready to run free,
but she makes us wait.
Stand in line.
High-five her.
Say goodbye.
Eye to eye.
Every single day.

I used to think it was weird,
but I guess I'm getting used
    to it.

She's still kind of weird,
though.
I guess I'm getting used to
    that, too.

▫ ▫ ▫ ▫

Today, her high-five face is
bigger
brighter
when it's my turn
for high five and bye.

Ben B.
You amaze me.
I had no idea,
no idea
how fast you could type.

For a minute I can't think
    of anything
at all
to say.
Then . . .

Do I type fast?

You do!
I'm quite impressed.
Quite impressed.
Of course I'd prefer
full sentences
and proper spelling,

but even so,
good work today.
Maybe we can think of
        other ways
for you to use your typing skills
in class.
Let's both think about that,
okay?

I feel my back straighten,
like a flower figuring out
which way
the sun shines.

Good at typing?
Huh.

□ □ □ □

I saw the lights behind Ms. J's
        eyes turn on,
just then,
and it felt almost like
she could see,
really see,
how being good at Sandbox

isn't just some dumb thing,
but an actual real thing,
an actual real thing I'm good at,
me
Ben B
and not just
BenBee.

□ □ □ □

Mom and Dad ask about
        my day
and I say
it was all right.
I don't want to tell them
        about reading,
about typing,
about anything.

Dad wants to see
my homework.
Mom wants to know
what I'm reading in class.
Dad wants to know
how FART prep
is coming along,

how I'm maximizing my time.
I let his voice drone,
try to ignore it,
try not to feel his questions
in my chest
like lead
weighing me down.

I want just a few more minutes
to feel the light, bright
shining feeling
of Ms J saying:
I'm quite impressed.
Quite impressed.
And knowing that she
    meant me.

ᒍHᗩT

Divergent Dingleberries

Private server created by: **BenBee**

Remember! Ghost Season is coming!

Password required

Avatar name:

Password:

Remember! Ghost Season is coming! Protect your lives, your health, and your gold by avoiding ghosts at all costs. Think you can outsmart the ghosts by logging out? Think again! All logged out avatars will remain in sleeping mode, so make sure you're protected. Get melted during Ghost Season? Gonna cost ya!

In order to bring you the very best game possible, Sandbox is moving to a pay-per-play model. Survive Ghost season? You'll maintain VIP status and continue on the free platform. Get melted? You can retrieve your gold and items when you sign up for one of our affordable monthly plans. Click here for more details.

OBenwhY ENTERS GAME

JORDANJMAGEDDON!!!!:

OBenwhY: hey Jordan

OBenwhY: u sure ran out of class fast

OBenwhY: after ur high five and bye

JORDANJMAGEDDON!!!!:

BenBee: ObenwhY heeeey.

OBenwhY: hey benbee I thought u were grounded from screens

BenBee: I am.

OBenwhY: then how are u here

BenBee: my parents go to sleep very early.

OBenwhY: sounds like ur playing with fire man

jajajavier:): hey look, ima fire man. i can juggle torches like a boss

OBenwhY: oh look who is magically able to talk

OBenwhY: u should prob put the torches down b4 u explode, javier

0BenwhY: ur standing right next to my dynamite amplifying potions

jajajavier:): what, no way they're going 2---

jajajavier:) HAS DIED
jajajavier:) HAS EXITED GAME

BenBee: omg

JORDANJMAGEDDON!!!!: 😂 😂 😂

0BenwhY: 😂 😂 😂

jajajavier:) ENTERS GAME

jajajavier:): ok fine, torch juggling was maybe 2 close 2 ur potions

BenBee: come on y'all, let's get to work on the pyramid.

0BenwhY: u said y'all! BenBeeeeeeee! u listened!!! ty

BenBee: 👍. now let's get going.

N00B8675309 ENTERS CHAT

BenBee: n00b? ur in the wrong place, bro.
BenBee: how did u even get in here? password protected, bro.

0BenwhY: not a n00b server, n00b

JORDANJMAGEDDON!!!!: 🙄

jajajavier:): Yeah! Go be n00by elsewhere, n00by Mcn00berson!

N00B8675309: Hello, I'm playing the game for the first time. I was hoping I could watch a little bit so that I could see how it---

CHAT INFRACTION

N00B8675309: Sorry, what just happened? Did I ask something that isn't allowed? It seems like pretty much anything is allow----

CHAT INFRACTION

N00B8675309: Is there a rulebook, somewhere? Maybe a manual that explains gameplay? That would be helpful, I think. Can someo----

CHAT INFRACTION.
N00B8675309 IS EJECTED FROM GAME.
THIRTY MINUTE RESPAWN COUNTDOWN BEGINS NOW.

JORDANJMAGEDDON!!!!:

jajajavier:): jajajajajajaja

jajajavier:): I took a screenshot of that mess jajajaja

0BenwhY: um that was super weird

BenBee: totally weird. i promise we're the only ones who know the password.

0BenwhY: it is kind of an easy pw tho

BenBee: wait.

0BenwhY: shouldn't be hard to change it

BenBee: no not that.
BenBee: the n00b back there.
BenBee: that wasn't

0BenwhY: what

BenBee: all those words and complete sentences. do u think it could've been

jajajavier:): straight up 100% Ms J pretending not to be Ms J?
jajajavier:): yes
jajajavier:): that's why I took the screenshot, nerd. so funny.

0BenwhY: WHUUUUUT omg did she just come here to SPY on us???

jajajavier:): well we did give her homework, so maybe not spying.
jajajavier:): maybe just researching
jajajavier:): maybe learning new skills from a very fantastic and handsome teacher

JORDANJMAGEDDON!!!!: ?

BenBee: i can't believe ms j infiltrated our home server.

JORDANJMAGEDDON!!!!:

BenBee: maybe she'll be better at sandbox than we thought.

BEN Y

<0benwhY>

I'm out of the house
before Esme wants hugs
and kisses
and her eyes
remind me
remind me
remind me.

Before Mom is up
asking
all
the
questions
about summer school
about where I've been,
all
the
questions
I don't feel like answering.

□ □ □ □

When these jeans were
Benicio's
he got holes
in all
the weirdest
places.

Was it his wallet chain
that rubbed this spot
raw?

Did his phone
sit so close
in this pocket
that the denim
wore away?

I haven't had them long
        enough
to make any holes
of my own.

But I will.
And these jeans will be ours.
Not just his story,
not just mine,
but something shared,
something worn.
Their unbinding
will be our tie
instead of the other way
around.

□ □ □ □

Hey, Jordan J.
What's hanging?
Scooch over, dude.

He starts talking
just like every day
when I get on the city bus
make him scooch
and we take the
extra
long
way
to school.

Jordan J.
The human version
of coffee.

Voice so happy,
it wakes me up.
Stories so funny,
I can't help but laugh.

He's always on the bus,
always way too early for school.

I never ask why.
It doesn't really matter.

He's always here.
And so am I.
We ride and chat,
and chat and ride.

I'm not sure
I can really explain why,
but it's nice.
Really nice.

I also can't explain why
it doesn't always translate
to school.

I actually don't mind
if it's different
when we're not on the bus.
That just makes the bus
a little more . . .
I don't know . . .
ours.

Our fun.
Our bus.
Our jokes.

Just a couple of moments
only
for
us.

□ □ □ □

Three of my strut strides,
equal two Jordan J
    dancing leaps
as we move from the bus stop,
making our way to school.

Part of our routine,
this sweaty duet
is swimming through the
    morning heat,
trying not to be too early,
not to be too late,
stretching out the minutes
    of freedom
before the stairwell,
before divergence
takes over the day.

Hey.

Jordan J twirls, a perfect
    pirouette,
points,
Javier by a white car,
leaning in the window.

Jordan J and I duck.
I don't know why
we hide
between the willow fronds,
forest bathing
as we spy.
But we do.

I w-w-w-w-w-won't!
N—No!
Javier is mad, shouting.
The wind catches words
coming from inside the car,
words like *help you*
and *it will be fine*
and *trust.*

Mom! N—No! I h-h-hate it.

Javier slams his fist
on the car door
where the window is rolled
down.

It doesn't h-help.
It m-makes me f-feel stu-stu—

He doesn't finish.
He storms away.

The woman in the car shouts:
Javier!
Come on! You're the smartest
    person I know!
Javier!

He whips around,
marches back to the car,
shouts:

S.T. is f-f-f-for
b-b-b-babies!

He pulls his hoodie
over his face.
Storms off into school.

Jordan J and I look at each
    other.

Is that why Javier won't talk?
I whisper,
swiping a tickly frond from
    my cheek.
Why he won't read out loud?
In class?
His stutter?

But we're all terrible at read-
ing out loud so that means he
wouldn't be any different than
any of us, maybe we should
just tell him that. Also, isn't he
really really really hot in that
hoodie? I mean sweaty hot,
not like movie-star hot. I am
sweating my I can't say off
and I'm wearing shorts and
this AWESOME Fierce Across
America tank top. Oh, oops,
are we still supposed to be
whispering? That wasn't really
a whisper was it? I'm not a
great whisperer.

I shrug.
Jordan J shrugs.

We sit under the tree.
Hmm.
Interesting.

▫ ▫ ▫ ▫

Like a shadow with a hoodie,
like a song stuck in my head
Javier
Javier
Javier.

When my eyes lock
with Javier's deep dark stare
in class,
I can't figure out . . .
what
is
he
thinking?
Did he see us under the tree?

Javier
Javier
Javier,
is it the stutter that makes you
    so quiet?

You're so funny in chat,
but now,
half hidden,
hoodie pulled tight,
you're a mystery,
and I can't help but wonder
can you see into *me*?
can mystery see mystery?

He blinks,
looks away,
head bowed,
pencil scratching,
always drawing,
never talking.

Javier
Javier
Javier,
can I see what you draw?

Javier
Javier
Javier,
what secrets do you know?

□ □ □ □

Three announcements!

Ms. J's voice is bright,
a yellow pop of sound
sparkling around us.

One!
My avatar is JJ11347.
It was supposed to be only
    JJ113
but I guess there are forty-six
    other JJ113s?
And the game added the
    forty-seven?
And I don't have enough gold
    to change my name yet?

The snickers tiptoe
up and down the walls,

until Jordan lets out a
    full-on snort
and we all collapse in laughs.

Ms. J is laughing, too,
when she claps again,
a firework pop
startling us quiet.

We gather up our laughs,
stuff them in our mouths,
try to swallow them
so we can see . . .
is her next announcement
as funny as the first?

□ □ □ □

Two!

Thank you to Javier,
who happened to be here
after school yesterday,
and who happened to stay
to help me muddle through
setup

after seeing how badly
I mucked up
my avatar name.

It is because of Javier
that we can play the actual
* game today.*
Can we all please give him
a round of quiet applause?

My eyes grow so wide
they might actually
    have merged
into one giant eye
that catches Ben B's matching
    giant eyes
and our eyes both say:

Because . . . what now?
Javier was here?
With her?
After school?
And does that mean?
She was chatting with us?
While they both were here?

So probably she didn't hack
    anything at all?
Because Javier let her into
    the server?

I clap very slowly and point my
    clap at Javier.
Ben B follows my lead.
Javier's cheeks turn pink,
and his mouth curls into a
devilish grin,
before Ms. J says,

Javier, all of your help means
*   you're reading today,*
correct?
You're playing today?
Yes?

Javier's grin disappears,
his face quickly bending,
trying to blend in with
his notebook.

▫ ▫ ▫ ▫

Three!

Please listen carefully:
When we chat during

typing practice,

everyone is to use
full sentences,
correct punctuation,
correct spelling.

I feel a moldy green groan
grow in my throat.

Please be advised
you all are very
very
very
lucky
to have

typing practice

in class.
Let's not groan too loudly

—she looks directly at me—

or we risk losing the privilege
altogether,
hmmmm?

Today's pink-and-gold caftan
shimmers
as her arms cross over her chest.

Good!

▫ ▫ ▫ ▫

Benita?
It's your turn to read.

I look down at the book
open on my desk,
pages fluttering
from the puffs of
almost cold air
drafting down and around
the stairs
and I get these feelings
all at once:

sadhappy
happysad
lovemad
madlove
hurtsmile
smilehurt
as I look
at the words;
in this Sandbox book
Benicio
would have loved.

It's Ben Y,
I say.

And I wonder
if wherever he is,
he can hear me,
if he knows
I've taken his name,
if he knows
everything
it means to me.

JORDAN

<JORDANJMAGEDDON!!!!>

I know Ms. J is very very new at Sandbox, but she is also very very bad at Sandbox even though apparently Javier stayed after school to help her. I feel kind of bad for her especially since she did her homework like we asked her to and she still got a bad avatar name and keeps running directly into walls like the Kool-Aid Man except not on purpose like the Kool-Aid Man.

□ □ □ □

There is one amazing thing about how Ms. J plays though and that is no matter how many walls she crashes into or how many cliffs she walks off of or how many times she walks in a circle because she doesn't understand the controls, she hasn't said one bad word or smashed her fists on the keyboard or anything. She keeps laughing and listening and saying *Jordan J please type words and sentences not just emojis, I don't understand where all your words have gone.* And then she gets a chat infraction and everyone yells CAREFUL and laughs a lot. And Ben Y says *Jordan J would use up all the words and leave none for us and also be the king of chat infractions if he didn't use only emojis. Plus also we need his big smart brain to think of cool things instead of being distracted by typing.*

□ □ □ □

Only, Ben Y doesn't say *exactly* that because hello that is way too many words which is a chat infraction just waiting to happen.

□ □ □ □

Chat infraction is the worst. Why did the game designers do that?

□ □ □ □

[fart noise]

□ □ □ □

omg omg omg omg omg omg omg omg omg Ms J just made that fart noise, not me NOT ME hahahahaha and now everyone is laughing so so hard because what! Ms J making a fart noise?! what! and now we are all making fart noises and Ms. J finally figured out how to use her pickax without stabbing Ben Y 4528452 times so we are all cheering extra loud and she says, *Shhhhhh this is* typing practice *you guys, no cheering in* typing practice but she's smiling and laughing and we are all so proud of her that no one yells at her for mining the diamonds out of the side of the pyramid we just built out of diamonds.

□ □ □ □

I saw Javier look up and smile really fast when the rest of us were laughing and I wish he would read out loud so he could play with us. Maybe there's something we can do to let him know that his stutter is fine and no one cares. I mean the rest of us are terrible at reading out loud and it sucks and we know how it feels to not want to do it but WE do it and that means he can too.

□ □ □ □

Ugh ugh speaking of things that no one wants to do but that we have to do sometimes, I just remembered that Mom asked me to go with her to the vet after school because Spartacus did not want to go for her morning walk today which was super weird because her morning walk is her favorite all time thing other than sneak attack leaping on my face when I eat ice cream. Except this morning she was asleep even when I said *Hey Spartacus, ready to roll* and when she woke up for a second she coughed a lot which is a thing I didn't know dogs could do until Spartacus started doing it a few months ago. It was kinda funny at first, *cough cough HWACK* like she had a super loogie, but it isn't funny anymore because it's all the time and it scares me and I really really really really don't want to go to the vet with Mom and now my brain feels like it has worry wrinkles in it and worry wrinkles are not my favorite because they trip up all my other thoughts and my other thoughts fall in the wrinkles which means that ALL my thoughts get trapped in the worry wrinkles and now all my thoughts will be worries about Spartacus.

□ □ □ □

Right, yeah, high five and bye, Ms. J. Yeah, yeah, everything is okay. Super cool no trouble at all nothing to see here move along. For real I'm fine. I'm definitely not thinking about Spartacus and I definitely do not have brain wrinkles or a stomachache right now. Nope definitely not any of those things.

□ □ □ □

Dang it's like she has some kind of x-ray vision that sees brain wrinkles, I don't even know but the way she looked at me was like laserlaserlasereyes into my face, but nice laser eyes, not evil super-hero laser eyes, and whew that was close because I almost said something about Spartacus but then I was like nahhhhh maybe don't do that, maybe let's not say any of this out loud, cool? Cool. So now I'm walking around the back of the school because maybe if I get home late I won't have to go with Mom to the vet and also dance team summer practice is about to start and yeah whatever I know I'm not on the dance team but that is one hundred percent Their Loss and they don't know that I can stand by the window in the gym door that's outside and by the trees and I can learn their moves and add better moves of my own and practice until it gets dark and Mom texts, *Jordan, where are you? Call me right now.*

▫ ▫ ▫ ▫

Dance moves all snap together like Legos, if you think about it, like you can see one Lego or one dance move and be like wait I don't think that Lego or dance move is going to jive with that other Lego or dance move, but then you find a little connector Lego or dance move that fits them both and joins them up snap snap snap, slide slide slide, all smooth-like and you go whoa whoa whoa check out how *this* looks, who would've known? But now YOU know because you're the linker-upper, you're the fitter-together-er. It's like my brain speaks a lot of weird languages other brains don't speak and dance is one of those languages. I mean I'm just dancing right here outside the gym, where no one can see me or tell me if I'm doing it right or doing it wrong, but I know it's right because my body knows the language and I stop for a second because I get my second brain wrinkle of the day imagining what my life would be like if I could figure out how letters and words and sentences fit together like limbs and bodies and spins.

JAVIER

<jajajavier:)>

142

CHAT

Divergent Dingleberries

Private server created by: **BenBee**

Password required

Avatar name:

Password:

Remember! Ghost Season is coming! Protect your lives, your health, and your gold by avoiding ghosts at all costs. Think you can outsmart the ghosts by logging out? Think again! All logged out avatars will remain in sleeping mode, so make sure you're protected. Get melted during Ghost Season? Gonna cost ya!

In order to bring you the very best game possible, Sandbox is moving to a pay-per-play model. Survive Ghost season? You'll maintain VIP status and continue on the free platform. Get melted? You can retrieve your gold and items when you sign up for one of our affordable monthly plans. Click here for more details.

BenBee: That looks really great, Ms. J. Keep it up.

JJ11347: Your sentences look really great, Ben B. Keep it up!

BenBee: It makes typing too slow.

JJ11347: We're going for accuracy, not speed, plus you're already lightning fast.In fact, let's talk after class about how—

CHAT INFRACTION

JJ11347: Argh! About how typing might help you IN class.

BenBee: Huh? I'm typing in class right now.

JJ11347: I mean, typing your notes. Typing your tests. Things like that.

0BenwhY: You know what's not fast?
0BenwhY: Your building skillz, Ms. J.
0BenwhY: tick tock

JJ11347: "Skills." Also, please put tick-tock in a complete sentence.

OBenwhY: omg

OBenwhY: I hear a tick tock in my brain clock that means we are all going to get melted because you are so slow the ghosts will—

CHAT INFRACTION

OBenwhY: aaargggh. Complete sentences ruin the game!!

JORDANJMAGEDDON!!!!: 😄

JJ11347: Please phrase that in the form of a sentence, Jordan J.

JORDANJMAGEDDON!!!!:
benygotachatinfractionanditwassofunnyomgshesjustlikeyou

JJ11347: Jordan J, that's your first warning today. Do you want to sit out?

JORDANJMAGEDDON!!!!: 😖

JJ11347: Jordan J! Do you want to sit out?

JORDANJMAGEDDON!!!!: Could I sit with Javier?

JJ11347: Good sentence, but don't test me. And no.

0BenwhY: Chat is so much funnier with Javier.

JJ11347: Well, Javier is going to have to start reading in class like everyone else.

JORDANJMAGEDDON!!!!: He's never going to read out loud because he stutters.

0BenwhY: JORDAN J! THAT'S NOT YOUR BUSINESS TO TELL!

JORDANJMAGEDDON!!!!: But its true. We should do something to show him he's normal and ok.

0BenwhY: omg, of course Javier is a normal person, Jordan. Who would think he wasn't???

JORDANJMAGEDDON!!!!: Well I mean *he* might.

JJ11347: Oh, Jordan J.

JORDANJMAGEDDON!!!!: ms j please do not look at me like your face is melting I'm telling the truth.

JORDANJMAGEDDON!!!!: we could all stand up to show our support like in the Spartacus movie except we could say I AM JAVI--

CHAT INFRACTION

JJ11347: I don't think that's exactly how that movie worked, Jordan J.

JJ11347: Speaking of how things work, how do I get a pork chop out of this pig?

JORDANJMAGEDDON!!!!: but everyone was brave an stood up for each other in that movie

JORDANJMAGEDDON!!!!: and that's why I named my dog Spartacus

JORDANJMAGEDDON!!!!: just kill it. with your pick ax.

JORDANJMAGEDDON!!!!: kill the PIG, not Ben Y!! Ben Y is not made of pork chops!

JORDANJMAGEDDON!!!!: Don't be a teacher griefer! Come on!

JJ11347: I apologize for stabbing you, Ben Y. These axes aren't easy to use.

JORDANJMAGEDDON!!!!: YES THEY ARE.

JJ11347: Please watch your tone, Jordan J.

JORDANJMAGEDDON!!!!: TYPING HAS A TONE?

JJ11347: Indeed it can. Please tap your caps lock button so that you stop shouting at me.

BenBee: so what can we do to help?

JORDANJMAGEDDON!!!!: Ms. J? Or me? She needs more lessons. I already hit the cap lock.

JORDANJMAGEDDON!!!!: oh, or do you mean Spartacus? Because she's sick?

BenBee: No no. Javier. What can we do to help Javier? Tho sorry to hear about Spartacus.

BenBee: I don't think Ms. J will ever get a pork chop.

JJ11347: Hey! Unfair! I am still learning!

JORDANJMAGEDDON!!!!: Now look whos shouting. Exclamation points mean shouting, too!

JJ11347: Jordan J, I'm learning you can be quite argumentative in chat.

JORDANJMAGEDDON!!!!: thank you.

JJ11347: That was not a compliment.

OBenwhY: let's all brainstorm tonight. and when it's Javier's turn to read tomorrow, boom, we show the love.

JORDANJMAGEDDON!!!!: 🖤 🖤 🖤 😥

OBenwhY: okay okay, back to it. We only have a few minutes left. Ms. J can you hold this?

JJ11347: Sure. What is it?

OBenwhY: Are you holding it? Okay.
OBenwhY: Push the up arrow on your keyboard fastly.

JJ11347: Fastly is not a word.
JJ11347: I'm pushing it.

OBenwhY: Keep doing it.

BenBee: More.

JJ11347: Ahhh! What just happened? What am I doing? Am I FLYING?

OBenwhY: Ha! You're doing it!

BenBee: Good job!

JORDANJMAGEDDON!!!!: 👏 GoodjobMsJNoRelation!

OBenwhY: You pooped your first fairy, Ms. J. Congratulations.

JORDANJMAGEDDON!!!!: Ms. J. pooped a fairy!!!!!!!!!!!!!!!!!!!!!!

JJ11347: I WHAT?

BenBee: hahahaha

OBenwhY: POPPED. POPPED.

OBenwhY: Popped a fairy! Killed it for the dust! So she can fly! Shut up!

JJ11347: Settle down. Settle down. I don't know how I feel about being a fairy killer. I wish the game designers had—

CHAT INFRACTION

BenBee: hahaha

JORDANJMAGEDDON!!!!: 😂 I mean, ha ha ha, I am laughing in full sentences.

OBenwhY: you're just doing it on purpose now, Ms. J, aren't you?

JJ11347: GAH. NO I AM NOT.

JORDANJMAGEDDON!!!!: i never do it on purpose either.

JJ11347: That was a lovely sentence, Jordan.

JJ11347: Wow! Am I already at the amusement park??

JJ11347: Is that the ocean??

BenBee: Fast and far. I'm still mad that wasn't a choice in the book. Totally worth fairy carnage.

JORDANJMAGEDDON!!!!: Totally worth pooping fairies, you mean?

JJ11347: This is a strange game.
JJ11347: Excellent sentence structure, Jordan J, but you are on thin ice.

0BenwhY: You're really good at flying, Ms. J.

JJ11347: Thank you, Benita. You're really good at this game. A master.
JJ11347: I am quite impressed.

0BenwhY: It's Ben Y. And you're getting better, you know.
0BenwhY: I think you might actually mine diamonds faster than me.
0BenwhY: one day you might even figure out how to eat a pork chop

JJ11347: Wow! Really?

0BenwhY: No! 😄

JJ11347: That's not very nice, Ben Y.

0BenwhY: Then why are you laughing?

JJ11347: That's the bell, kids. Pack up your stuff
JJ11347: Hey, Ben Y. How do I get out of this tree?

0BenwhY HAS EXITED GAME
JORDANJMAGEDDON!!!! HAS EXITED GAME

JJ11347: Can someone help me out of this tree? Ben B?
JJ11347: Ben B?

BenBee HAS EXITED GAME

JJ11347: Fine. I'll figure it out myself.

Divergent Dingleberries

Private server created by: **BenBee**

Password required

Avatar name:

Password:

Remember! Ghost Season is coming! Protect your lives, your health, and your gold by avoiding ghosts at all costs. Think you can outsmart the ghosts by logging out? Think again! All logged out avatars will remain in sleeping mode, so make sure you're protected. Get melted during Ghost Season? Gonna cost ya!

In order to bring you the very best game possible, Sandbox is moving to a pay-per-play model. Survive Ghost season? You'll maintain VIP status and continue on the free platform. Get melted? You can retrieve your gold and items when you sign up for one of our affordable monthly plans. Click here for more details.

JORDANJMAGEDDON!!!!: is it just me or is it starting to feel weird?

OBENWHY: is what starting to feel weird?

JORDANJMAGEDDON!!!!: not having Ms. J in chat with us all the time.
JORDANJMAGEDDON!!!!: like, here we are, hanging by the chickenfall, and she's not here.

OBENWHY: you want to be chatting with your teacher after dinner?
OBENWHY: when we're not even in school?
OBENWHY: and after we already chatted with her for ten whole minutes in class?
OBENWHY: *that* is weird.

JORDANJMAGEDDON!!!!: i don't know. maybe. but she's kind of funny in a dumb way.
JORDANJMAGEDDON!!!!: i don't mean dumb in a mean way.
JORDANJMAGEDDON!!!!: wait. look at that. ^^ how many meanings does mean have?

OBENWHY: JORDAN J STAY ON TASK. WHY DID YOU ASK US ALL HERE?

JORDANJMAGEDDON!!!!: I want you all to trust me, ok. the I AM JAVIER thing is a great idea.

OBENWHY: is it?

JORDANJMAGEDDON!!!!: ❓ why not?

OBENWHY: i don't know, he seems kind of like a private dude
OBENWHY: what if we embarrass him

JORDANJMAGEDDON!!!!: we're not embarrassing him! We're helping him! just like when spartacus helps all the people to

CHAT INFRACTION

JORDANJMAGEDDON!!!!: 😖

BenBee ENTERS CHAT

BenBee: hey hey hey, how's that pyramid looking
BenBee: i see its looking . . . exactly the same as it did last night
BenBee: ghost season approacheth, y'all. we are going to be shiitake out of luck without shelter

JORDANJMAGEDDON!!!!: shiitake what? isn't that a 🍄? hahahaha

OBENWHY: 100% 🍄 out of luck unless someone knows the ghostkiller potion

BenBee: hardee har har, if only that potion was real

OBENWHY: it's totally real

JORDANJMAGEDDON!!!!: i feel like we're getting off topic

OBENWHY: oh look who's on topic all of a sudden 😜
OBENWHY: i get it, we want to help Javier read in class. like, feel comfortable or whatever
OBENWHY: also i never ever ever want to read more than my fair share ever again
JORDANJMAGEDDON!!!!: that's what i'm saying! if all of us y'alls help javier, then he'll read and no one has to double

CHAT INFRACTION

JORDANJMAGEDDON!!!!: 😖 😖 😖 up their own reading
JORDANJMAGEDDON!!!!: plus also he can play sandbox in class which would be awesome so lets get all Spartacus up in here

CHAT INFRACTION
JORDANJMAGEDDON!!!! IS EJECTED FROM GAME
THIRTY MINUTE RESPAWN COUNTDOWN BEGINS

BenBee: just tell me what the plan is and i'll help. for now tho, can we

BenBee: please

BenBee: build

BenBee: this

BenBee: frickin

BenBee: frackin

BenBee: pyramid

BenBee: oh shiitake mushrooms, my dad is coming up the stairs i have to go

BenBee HAS EXITED GAME

OBENWHY: i rly am surrounded by dingleberries.

BEN B

<BenBee>

It feels strange.

The same,
but different.

Different but,
familiar.

The keyboard
under my fingers.

My fingers
typing words.

Not Sandbox words, though.
Not chat words.

Assignment words.
Spelling. Grammar. Notes.

And it's nice.

(Not nice, like
fun nice,
or Sandbox nice.
But nice, like
brain and fingers agreeing nice.
Not stressful nice.)

Easy nice.

▫ ▫ ▫ ▫

Do not
let me catch you
doing anything
anything .
but schoolwork.

That's what she said,
after school,
yesterday,
when we talked about
how typing my notes
and tests and stuff
in class
might be a super great thing
to try.

I'll make a note,
in your file,
about this accommodation.
And if the typing helps,
when school starts in the fall,
you can get something
    called a 504

so that you can type in
every class.

She pointed at me.

No games.
Only schoolwork.

I shook her finger,
like you shake someone's hand.
Deal.

We both laughed
and I felt lighter somehow,
brighter somehow,
like a light I didn't know
was there
had finally been
switched on.

□ □ □ □

Art Class Monday.
Soccer Practice Tuesday.
FART Tutoring Wednesday.
Handwriting Thursday.
Piano Lessons Friday.
Soccer Game Saturday.
House Cleaning Sunday.

Everything is still the same.
Nothing there has changed.
That's how it is.
That's how it was.
That's how it will be.
My days of the week.
My path to greatness.

Typing has never been part of it.
But now I wonder . . .
could typing be the key
Mom and Dad have been
searching for?
The thing that finally
makes me,
Ben B,
perfectly
lined up
typed up
smart?

Can I finally
be good at something?

Huh.

□ □ □ □

BEN Y

<0BenwhY>

Today.

I open my eyes
look up at the ceiling,
as Esme reads softly,
her voice drifting up
from the bottom bunk.

Benicio looks down,
his half smile
crooked,
hiding his deep voice,
hiding . . .
so much.

I reach up,
touch the photo taped to
    the ceiling,
notice the colors,
they've started to fade,
a year of sunlight
sneaking through the window,
trying to take him from me
again.

I close my eyes.
My morning breath
catches
in my chest.

It's coming.
The anniversary.
I feel it breathing down
        my neck,
I feel it sitting on my chest.

Even Esme's sweet voice
can't calm my jumping
        stomach,
can't find answers to the whys
that swirl around me,
making me dizzy
as I look at them
and wish I could find
their answers.

▫ ▫ ▫ ▫

Lucky for me,
I have an excuse
to run from my room,

to burst into the sunlight,
to fly onto the bus
and
ride
ride
ride
far away
from my room,
my house,
my sisters,
my mother.

Can't be late for school, right?
Even summer school, right?
And today's a big day,

the Javier day,
the day we're going to get
    him to read,
the day we show him
he has nothing to run from,
nothing to hide,
that we're here for him,
and . . .

whoa
whoa
oh man.
I hate it when out of nowhere,
I start to cry.

JORDAN J

<JORDANJMAGEDDON!!!>

Okay okay okay we are about to Spartacus Javier. This is it, this is what we talked about, this is when Javier is going to see how he's just as good or as bad or whatever at reading as the rest of us, because sure we're all different like how Ben B has two different colored eyes but also we're all the same like how reading out loud feels basically the same as standing naked on a stage, or how I would imagine it, anyway. We are going to Spartacus Javier and it is going to be even more awesome than when all those people yell out I AM SPARTACUS in the movie so that the bad guys can't find him. If this was a movie I guess the book would be the bad guy? And all the words in it would see that we are all the same and they can't beat any of us and this is so exciting I can barely breeeeeeeeeeeeathe, here we go!

□ □ □ □

Javier is always hiding behind his hoodie so I have to lean over and peek into it as soon as I'm done reading and I say *Have you seen the movie Spartacus? Can we all Spartacus you to help you read out loud?* And he looks at me like I am wearing that diaper thing Spartacus wears and then I say *Come on trust me, that movie has never steered me wrong and we all know you want to play Sandbox in class, plus we miss you when you don't play so let us help you read out loud. Pleasepleasepleasepleasepleaepleasepleasepleaseplease.* And Javier looks so confused he almost makes me laugh except he picks up the book from his desk and stands up and holy cats I can't believe this is happening.

□ □ □ □

Javier! Starts! Reading! Out! Loud!

▫ ▫ ▫ ▫

Ms. J looks like Spartacus (the dog, not the movie guy) when Spartacus thinks she's hiding but she's really standing in the middle of the
kitchen waiting for you to drop a piece of cheese, and everyone else
is holding their breath, too and Javier says *D-d-d—* and I know he's
going to say the word *do* because I can see it in my book, so I shout

DO!

I AM JAVIER!

so that way Javier knows that I know what it's like to be standing
there having a hard time with a word and also so that the words know
that we are all the same and they can't beat us down and now Javier
looks at me like whut before dipping his head back to the book and
reading with his deep, deep man-voice, *Y-y-y*, and I whack Ben Y
in the arm because it's her turn now.

▫ ▫ ▫ ▫

Ben Y yells out *YOU* and then *I AM JAVIER*, but not as loud as I
yelled mine and oh boy those words know who's the boss now. They
know we're all in this together and we're all the same as Javier even
though no one else has a stutter and now Javier is giving his whut
look to Ben Y and Ben Y is taking his whut look and adding a little

bit of a huh to it and she's flinging that huh whut look at me, but whatever, this is working and it is awesome and now Javier's deep, deep man-voice says, *Ch-ch-ch—* and I point at Ben B because it's his turn now and my heart is pounding so hard because we are all Javier, we really really are, and he is getting to see it and it's just like we're in the movie.

□ □ □ □

Ben B looks in his book and shouts CHOOSE, and then he shouts I AM JAVIER and there's this energy in the room like we are all onstage and it's the final dance of *Fierce Across America* and Veronica Verve is about to announce the winner and we all know that we are all the winner because we are all Javier and I can't help but laugh a tiny bit and jump up and down a tiny bit even though Ben B and Ms. J have added some extra huhs and whuts onto the huh whut look and Javier adds some pointy eyebrows and a mouth so scrunched up it looks like a cat butt and he points it right at me as he smashes his book onto his desk WHAM, grabs his stuff, and runs out of the room.

□ □ □ □

Wait.

□ □ □ □

What just happened?

JAVIER

`<jajajavier:)>`

THEY AREN'T ME, NOT EVEN CLOSE. HOW COULD THEY THINK THEY'RE ME? DO THEY KNOW ME? DO THEY UNDERSTAND MY LIFE?

NO NO NO

NONE

OF

ARE THEY JUST MAKING FUN OF ME?

YES YES YES YES YES YES YES YES YES YES

THEM

I DIDN'T THINK THEY WERE MEAN.

IT'S SO MEAN TO MAKE FUN

ARE ME

 CHAT

Divergent Dingleberries

Private server created by: **BenBee**

Password required

Avatar name:

Password:

Remember! Ghost Season is coming! Protect your lives, your health, and your gold by avoiding ghosts at all costs. Think you can outsmart the ghosts by logging out? Think again! All logged out avatars will remain in sleeping mode, so make sure you're protected. Get melted during Ghost Season? Gonna cost ya!

In order to bring you the very best game possible, Sandbox is moving to a pay-per-play model. Survive Ghost season? You'll maintain VIP status and continue on the free platform. Get melted? You can retrieve your gold and items when you sign up for one of our affordable monthly plans. Click here for more details.

JORDANJMAGEDDON!!! ENTERS GAME

JORDANJMAGEDDON!!!: no one here.

JORDANJMAGEDDON!!!: too early after school?

JORDANJMAGEDDON!!!: i can wait

JORDANJMAGEDDON!!!: i can wait

JORDANJMAGEDDON!!!: i'll wait forever

JORDANJMAGEDDON!!!: a million years

JORDANJMAGEDDON!!!: there won't be a game anymore

JORDANJMAGEDDON!!!: but i'll still be here

JORDANJMAGEDDON!!!: to say i'm sorry

JORDANJMAGEDDON!!!: even though i don't really get it

JORDANJMAGEDDON!!!: we were really Spartacusing so well

JORDANJMAGEDDON!!!: and we were showing those words
that WE have the power

JORDANJMAGEDDON!!!: and i don't understand

JORDANJMAGEDDON!!!: why that made Javier so mad

JORDANJMAGEDDON!!!: but it definitely did and

JORDANJMAGEDDON!!!: and I definitely feel bad and
confused and then bad again

JORDANJMAGEDDON!!!: i am doing such a good job of
not getting a chat infraction and no one is even
here to see it--

CHAT INFRACTION

JORDANJMAGEDDON!!!: what! no way! how was that too
many characters???

JJ11347 ENTERS GAME

JORDANJMAGEDDON!!!: oh hey, ms j.

JORDANJMAGEDDON!!!: wait. why are you here? this isn't school.

JORDANJMAGEDDON!!!: teachers don't chat or play sandbox with students after dinner, do they?

JJ11347: Hi, Jordan. You're right, I don't want to interfere with you all while you're playing in the evenings. But today—

CHAT INFRACTION

JORDANJMAGEDDON!!!: 😂 we're the same, Ms. J! Haha. Too many words.

JJ11347: Too many words, and yet we both have trouble finding the right ones, sometimes, don't we? Have you talked to Javi--

CHAT INFRACTION

JJ11347: Oh, come on.

JORDANJMAGEDDON!!!: i know! chat infraction is the serious worst

JORDANJMAGEDDON!!!: i haven't talked to Javier, but i wish i could so i could say sorry

JORDANJMAGEDDON!!!: do you know why he got so mad, though? we were helping him

JORDANJMAGEDDON!!!: i know he wants to play sandbox in class

JORDANJMAGEDDON!!!: and ben y and i figured out the stuttering thing

JORDANJMAGEDDON!!!: and I thought that Spartacusing him would be perfect, but

JORDANJMAGEDDON!!!: ugh

JORDANJMAGEDDON!!!: we just wanted to help him

JJ11347: When someone has a different ability, like dysfluency, it's good to ask before you try to help

JJ11347: Did you ask Javier first?

JORDANJMAGEDDON!!!: no. we, well, i, wanted to kind of surprise him with it

JJ11347: I appreciate that you were trying to help, but you know what your next steps are, right? You know what y—

CHAT INFRACTION
JJ11347 HAS BEEN EJECTED FROM THE GAME
THIRTY MINUTE RESPAWN COUNTDOWN BEGINS NOW

JORDANJMAGEDDON!!!: yes, i know.

JORDANJMAGEDDON!!!: that's why i'm here

JORDANJMAGEDDON!!!: i need to say i'm sorry

JORDANJMAGEDDON!!!: so i'll wait

JORDANJMAGEDDON!!!: until Javier shows up

JORDANJMAGEDDON!!!: and Ben B and Ben y

JORDANJMAGEDDON!!!: i'll wait forever

JORDANJMAGEDDON!!!: to say sorry

JORDANJMAGEDDON!!!: maybe ms. j will come back and I can do a good deed

JORDANJMAGEDDON!!!: to make up for my accidental bad deed

JORDANJMAGEDDON!!!: maybe i can help ms. j get a pork chop

JORDANJMAGEDDON!!!: just help and help and help

JORDANJMAGEDDON!!!: and stay here

JORDANJMAGEDDON!!!: in Mom's office

JORDANJMAGEDDON!!!: because Spartacus

JORDANJMAGEDDON!!!: the dog not the movie guy

JORDANJMAGEDDON!!!: is coughing so much

JORDANJMAGEDDON!!!: i can't hear Dance Across America

JORDANJMAGEDDON!!!: and that makes me nervous in two ways

JORDANJMAGEDDON!!!: and this Javier thing makes me nervous in another way and so i'm just feeling really nervous right now and

CHAT INFRACTION

JORDANJMAGEDDON!!! HAS BEEN EJECTED FROM GAME

THIRTY MINUTE RESPAWN COUNTDOWN BEGINS NOW

0BenwhY ENTERS GAME

0BenwhY: anyone here?

0BenwhY: that is an epic chat log

0BenwhY: whoa

BenBee ENTERS GAME

BenBee: hello?

BenBee: what did i miss?

0BenwhY: hey, Ben B. check out the chat log.

BenBee: hey.

BenBee: oh wow.

BenBee: you want to wait with me until he respawns?

0BenwhY: we do have this pyramid to finish.

BenBee: yep. if we don't save ourselves, no one
else will.

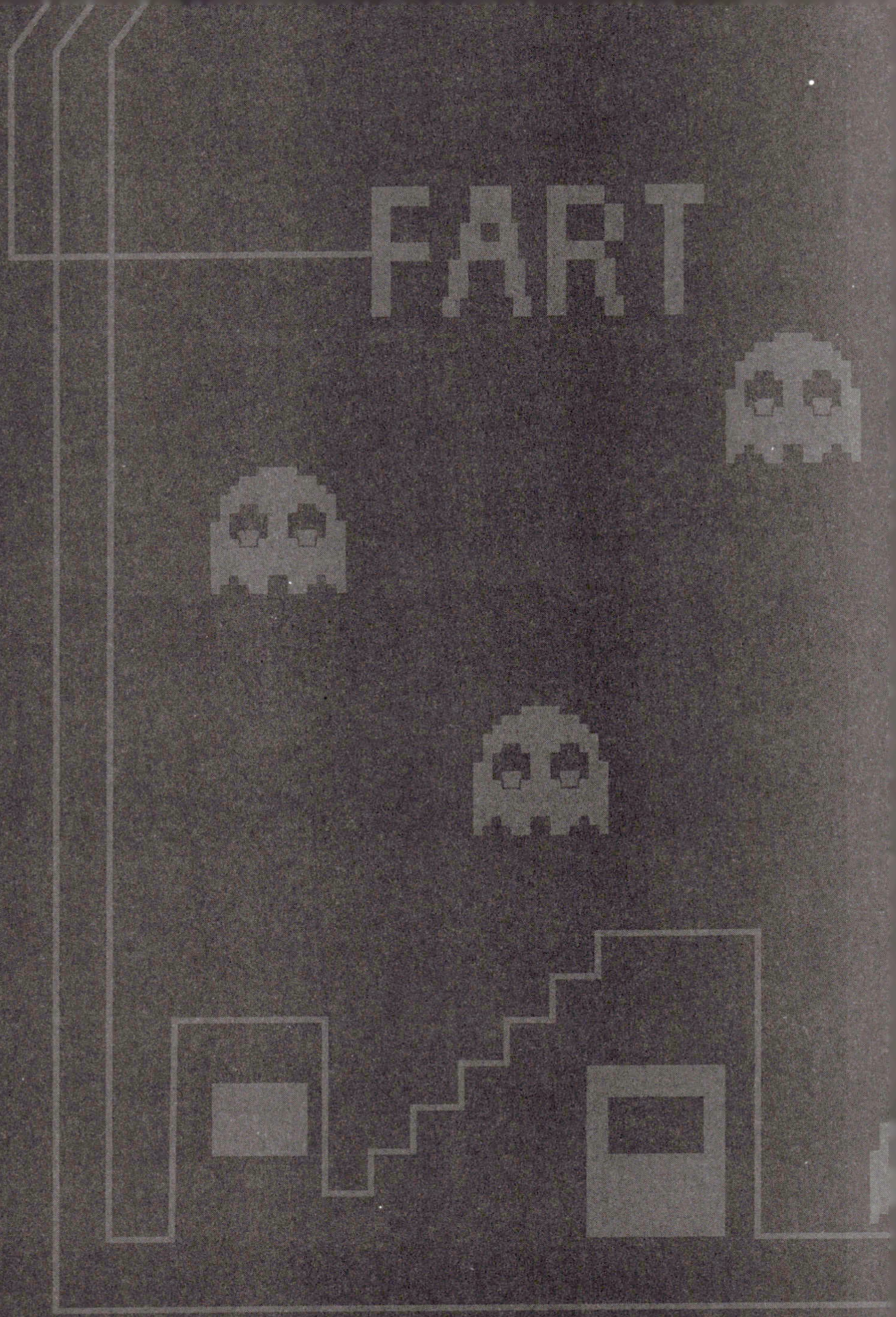
FART

<Part II>

SAVE UR SELF

Congratulations! You have survived ghosts and surprise enemies and even the elements! (Brrr, it got cold there for a little while, didn't it? Good thing you made those extra torches!) You might think you have developed the skillz and intuition to move through the rest of your adventure with ease. But! If you did think this, you would be in trouble. That's right, the toughest part of your journey awaits:

The battle to save ur self!

To join forces with the nearest guild, turn to **page 105**.

To stay with your current rag-tag set of "allies", turn to **page 130**.

From *Save Ur Server, Save Ur Self: A Many Choices Sandbox Adventure Book* by Tennessee Williamson

BEN B

<BenBee>

You're doing great.
Look at all those notes!

Her words echo
echo
echo
in my brain.

I'm doing great?

I look at the words on
    the screen.
The letters all line up,
not huge and wiggly,
not scattered on the page.
These are real people words.
Anyone words.

The letters are neat.
They're perfectly shaped.
No hand cramps from a pencil,
nobody saying quietly
I write like I'm still in first grade.

Perfect words,
and they came from me.
From me.

She might be right.
I might be finally
for once
doing great.

▫ ▫ ▫ ▫

High five and bye.
High five and bye.
High five and bye.

She doesn't let go,
at the end of our high five,
instead she squeezes
once
twice.

I want to set up a meeting,
she says,
with your mom and dad.

I think we can work together,
try to get you a 504.
Do you remember what t
    hat is?

A voice echoes from above:
Jeans?

We both look up.
Ben Y leans over the stairs,
grinning
like a goof.

No, Ben Y.
Goodbye, Ben Y.
Please stop
eavesdropping, Ben Y.
Ms. J pulls me to her desk,
hands me a folded note.

We can start the process now,
so your teachers next year
have to let you type.

Have *to?*

Ms. J smiles.

Yes.
By law.
Now, it won't be in place
    this summer,
but your typing
accommodation is in your file.
I'll make sure admin grants
    you permission

to use the computer
for your retake.

Whoa, whoa.
What.

I can type *my FART retake*
answers?

Hey! Not fair!

Ms. J and I snap our heads up,
Ben Y's head still
leans down.

Ben Y!
GOOOD BYYYYEEEE!

Ms. J doesn't wave,
she shoos her hand at Ben Y,
who laughs and runs off.

Give this to your parents, okay?
We'll set up a meeting,
get the process started.

I'm not even sure what to say.
It doesn't feel real.

She holds up her hand.
Can I have an extra high five
and bye?

I slap her hand,
and let her squeeze mine
for one more second.

High five and bye, Ms. J.
I round the corner,
out of the stairwell,
but lean back
just a little bit,
and see her
gathering up papers.

Ms. J?

She looks up.

Thank you.

And then I run
before I can see her face.

▫ ▫ ▫ ▫

I lie in the grass,
stare up through the
willow fronds,
wonder where Javier is.
It's been two whole days now.

I've missed the bus.
Dad will be mad
to have to come pick me up.

But.

Even with the Javier stuff
clouding the edges of my mind,
I'm still savoring this minute
of nothing,
a gobstopper on my tongue.

A 504, huh?
Typing every day?
It *does* sound like jeans.
It sounds like a comfortable fit,
sized perfectly just for me.

BEN Y

<0BenWhy>

Can I help you, Benita?

Ms. J stops in the hallway.
She tilts her head to the side,
her earring hoop landing on
    her shoulder,
twisting just like a Jordan J
    pirouette.

Early evening light
pushes through high dusty
    windows,
rolls over lockers,
makes the hallway glow,
apparently
erasing the shadow
I snuggled into
after I finished spying.

It's Ben Y.
And, actually,
I was looking for you.

Wait. Was I?
Why would my mouth say that
before my brain could catch up?

Is my dino butt brain back?
Protecting me
before my real brain kicks in?

Ms. J's eyebrows
meet wrinkle speed bumps
as they slowly climb
the stumbly cliff
of her forehead.

She doesn't say anything.
Her starfish-shaped dress
matches the orange light,
catches the glow,
looking like Esme's cheeks
when she puckers around a
    flashlight,
trying to be a reverse firefly.

It's just . . . I've been thinking. I
    can tell you're working hard,
and don't get me wrong,
you're definitely getting
    better, just . . .
you could still use some
Sandbox help.

I keep my eyes on her eyes.
She keeps her eyes on my eyes.
Am I bluffing?
Am I not?
Even I don't know.
I just don't want to go home.

Maybe you need,
I don't know,
some after-school tutoring?

Ms. J sucks her bottom lip,
watches me stumble over
    my words.
She looks down at her watch.
She looks back up at me.

It's getting late.

I look at my wrist,
where a watch would be.
I look up at her.

It's never too late to get better
at Sandbox.

I give her my *just joking,*
mostly, crooked smile.

Those eyebrows again.
This time the wrinkle speed
bumps
don't slow them down at all.

Twenty minutes.
That's all I have before I
    need to go.

I nod,
follow her down the hall,
and think,
okay real brain,
okay dino butt brain,
we don't have to go home
right this second,
but . . .
now what?

▫ ▫ ▫ ▫

It's a little weird with just us
back under the stairs,
sitting next to each other
like we're both students.

Ms. J turns in her seat,
looks at me hard,
all the way through my eyes,
into the soft self
that tries so hard
to hide.

Then . . .
her eyes change;
the corners frown just a
    little bit,
but not in a bad way.
It's like they're matching
    the softness
they just saw in me.

Hey. Are you okay?

Her voice is as soft as her eyes,
and I feel something crack.
I've been working so hard

to hold everything together
and now . . .
I don't know,
I feel like,
right here,
right now,
I can't do it anymore.
How can such a soft voice,
such soft eyes . . .
how can they split me open
so fast?

Pain.
Sadness.
It drips out of me,
impossible to contain,
like trying to put a raw egg
back in its shell,
a shattered mess,
impossibly crushed,
broken.
She doesn't say anything,
just hands me a tissue
and watches
as I mop up the dripping bits,
as best I can.

Then
we play Sandbox.
No talking.
No lessons.
No tutoring.
Just playing.
For way longer
than twenty minutes.

□ □ □ □

She's actually pretty good now.

You've been practicing,
I type.

So have you, Ms. Apostrophe,
she types back.

I don't know why
this dripping moment,
this day,
this now,
is suddenly the right time,
but her eyes tell me it's okay,
something about her
whispers to me,
it's . . . safe

to sit with her,
to be with her.
To trust her.

So.

I say:

Hey.
You want to learn a trick?
It's really cool.
No one else in the entire world
can do it.
Only me.
And maybe you, I guess.
If you pay attention.

□ □ □ □

OBenwhY finds everything we
need,
JJ11347 watches carefully,
learning.

Just like he did.
Just like I did.
Almost a year ago.

OBenwhY helps JJ11347 find
    the things, too.
She makes her practice
    the potion
over and over.

Just like he did.
Just like I did.
Almost a year ago.

Look at you,
I say.
Just like he said to me,
his mahogany voice
smooth as ever.

You know the secret now.
What do you think?

▫ ▫ ▫ ▫

I watch her smile
grow wide wide wide as
    she says,
Wait. You can kill ghosts?
Forever?
But Ben B said that was
legend—

He said—

He's wrong.
I roll my eyes.

Her laugh is
not deep mahogany,
but still rich, smooth,
and I hold on to it,
tuck it away,
while she yells
TAKE THAT,
as she splashes all the ghosts
and they disappear,
except the one in my head,
in my heart,
in my bones,
in my blood,
my brother,
Benicio.
The first Ben Y.
The real Ben Y.
The biggest why
I've ever had
in my whole
entire
life.

▫ ▫ ▫ ▫

I watch her rampage,
killing every ghost in sight.

Ghostkiller.
The holiest of grails.
The most magical hack.
Alive again.
Brought back
to life.

It's the first time I've seen the
    potion since . . .
since he taught me,
since he passed it on,
since he passed on,
and what does it mean?
That I just showed her?
Right here?
Right now?

The potion only he could make,
the secret he shared with me,
as if he knew his car would
    crash,
as if he knew our last moment
was right then, that hour, that
    minute,
that day.

Splash a ghost
and the ghost sizzles into
    nothing.

Crash your car
and so do you.

But when you crash your car,
you don't have extra lives
saved, stored up, hoarded.
You have nothing,
nothing,
that can blink you
back to life.

▫ ▫ ▫ ▫

I don't know what Ms. J knows
about Ghostkiller.
I don't know if she understands
what I've shown her.

I don't tell her how famous
    he was.
I don't tell her about the VIPs
sending condolences,
about the developers
dedicating a bench

in Benicio's name
at their corporate offices
four states away.

I guess she already knows
that some people,
like Ben B,
think Ghostkiller was
    never real,
that he's a myth, a fake,
designed to get more people
    to play.

I don't tell her others think
    he's still alive,
but trapped inside the game.

I don't tell her he's in a box
in my house
on the bookshelf,
that he's dust now,
which is almost like sand,
which means he's become
almost his own
personal
sandbox

and maybe that would make
    him happy
finally
after not being happy
for so long.

I don't say any of that,
but I do fold this moment
    around me,
a soft, safe blanket in time.
I pull these quiet minutes close,
I snuggle into them,
breathing deep,
and I let myself
for once
feel the feelings
as they come,
instead of running
hard and fast
to get away from them.

I lean into Ms. J's soft eyes,
her soft words,
the soft light.
I let the words
I've been trying to outrun
finally win the race.

I look up at her,
as I pull this moment
even tighter
the soft blanket of now
becoming a bandage
holding together
the crack in my heart.

I say,
A year ago tomorrow
my brother died.
He was twenty-two.
He was the real Ghostkiller.
He was the one who
    programmed this trick,
the only person who knew it,
until he taught it to me,
like an hour
before his car crashed.

▫ ▫ ▫

She puts one hand
very very very lightly
on my shoulder,
never taking her eyes

from my eyes.
She nods.

I have no words,
except
Thank you.
Thank you for trusting me
    with this,
Benita.

And just like that,
everything crashes
all around me
and I realize how stupid
stupid
stupid
stupid
I am
to have shared any of this
    with her.

Her hand, still on my shoulder,
squeezes a tiny bit, as her
    voice lowers
an even tinier bit,
and she says,

Are you okay?
Is there someone I can call
    for you?
Benita?

▫ ▫ ▫ ▫

Benita?!
Benita?!
How many times . . . ?!
How
many
times
have I told her it's not Benita?
How
many
times
have I told her it's Ben Y?????

Benita. Hey. It's okay.
You can talk to me.

Doesn't she see?
Doesn't she realize?
If she keeps calling me Benita
it means
she doesn't hear me,
she doesn't see me

even though I'm right here
in front of her
shattering all over the place?

I'm right here
and she doesn't see me.

I just broke open my heart,
shared my biggest pain,
revealed the Ghostkiller secret,

and
she
still
can't
even
see
me
for
who
I
actually
am.

My brain melts down.
I don't know who
or what
controls me now,

but I know for sure
it isn't
frick
frackin'

Benita.

▫ ▫ ▫ ▫

Stop calling me that!

My voice is so loud it cracks.

It's Ben Y, okay?!
Not Benita.
Never Benita again.
It's Ben Y.
Ben Y.
WHY
can't
you
get
that
through
your
THICK
skull?!

Then
I'm running.
Fast and far.
Past the first bus stop.
Past the second.
Maybe I'll keep running,
until my legs fall off
until my heart explodes.

Why did I tell her anything?
Why did I do that?
Why did I feel safe?
Why am I so
dumb,
dumb,
dumb?

It's dark now.
I stop running.
I wait for the 315,
for it to take me across town,
for it to take me away
for it to take me anywhere
    but home
or here.

▫ ▫ ▫ ▫

A flash of bright white
as the bus door slides open,
making me squint and stumble
up the stairs.

All the whys of the day
    come at me,
pinpricking my mind,
coming alive,
taunting me,
giving me feelings
I can't even name.

The bus starts to move,
I blink back to now,
I trip over a foot,
crash into a seat.

Ow!
OhBenWhy did you just fall
    on top of me?

Jordan J's voice is as loud as
    the lights,
as I slide off him and onto
    the seat.

What are you doing here?

JORDAN J

(JordanJmageddon!!!!)

Ben Y just totally fell on me on the bus right now out of nowhere, how wild is that? Just splat on my lap like a giant tossed her at me, like she was a bowling ball and I was a pin and now she's looking at me like whut whut and I'm looking at her like whut whut and it's a whut whut fest.

▫ ▫ ▫ ▫

Ben Y is sort of in her own quiet time bubble right now which is weird to me, since she just fell on me and squished me. Also, she isn't asking any questions and she didn't answer MY question about why she's here and so, as my mom might say, that *concerns* me. I feel *concerned*. I have a *concern* about Ben Y and why she's here and why she isn't Why-ing.

▫ ▫ ▫ ▫

I am, in fact, on this bus because of another *concerning* thing, and that is the fact that Spartacus the dog, not the movie guy, is at peak sick right now, like if sick was a mountain she would be on top of it waiting for a helicopter to rescue her like that guy who climbed that mountain in the place where those cool camel-goats live. Spartacus is very very very sick and it was too *concerning* to be in my house right now with my mom and dad and sister and the vet tech who might be the helicopter rescuing Spartacus off of Peak Sick or might be helping Spartacus die peacefully at this very second or maybe that's the same thing and I really really do NOT want to know that.

▫ ▫ ▫ ▫

When I got kicked out of Sandbox for a stupid chat infraction I went into the kitchen to ask mom whycome nice things can turn into mean things by accident and I walked past the living room and I saw the vet tech's face, the serious slash of her mouth as she listened to Spartacus cough and cough, and it made me feel hot and melty in a very bad way inside my guts and I had to walk outside and get a fresh breath in my lungs because I thought I might throw up but then my feet needed a walk and it started to get dark and I might not be the smartest kid in the world, but also I know I don't want to get squished by a truck or even a small car so I got on the bus when I saw it stop. And now I just got squished by a Ben Y but that's okay because now there's someone to ride the bus with me while it loops through town over and over and I wish the squeals and groans of the bus noises could fill up my head, but they don't and I can still hear Spartacus gasping for breath and I can see the vet tech's mouth in its very serious shape and riding the bus isn't stopping any of that from replaying over and over in my head like the worst autoplay feature of all time which is saying something because all autoplay is basically garbage's garbage.

□ □ □ □

Also even though I can imagine Mom's *concern* that she doesn't know where I am, I still can't seem to get off the bus.

□ □ □ □

Spartacus is sick, I say to Ben Y even though she didn't ask. I just guessed that she would probably ask if she wasn't in her weird quiet bubble, so I might as well answer her anyway, right? Of course right. I don't really want to think about Spartacus but also Spartacus is the only thing I CAN think about. I don't want to think about her dying. I don't want to think about anything dying. I don't want to think about people dying or plants dying or even things that can't die dying. Like this bus or my shoes or Ben Y's pants with the holes in them. I know pants can't DIE die, but it makes me sad to think about her pants eventually having too many holes and getting thrown out. That's kind of like dying for pants and any kind of dying makes me sad. Especially animals dying. Especially Spartacus. And now I'm feeling concerned again. A lot of *concern* all at once and maybe some of it just leaked out of my eyes?

▫ ▫ ▫ ▫

Yes. Some of my *concern* leaked out of my eyes.

▫ ▫ ▫ ▫

Ben Y picks up my phone from the bus seat and she types something on it which is weird because how does she know my passcode but then I remember I changed my passcode so that it would be the same as the password to the dingleberry server so that I would stop forgetting all the password codes, and that was a very good guess on her part, good job detective Ben Y She pulls the ding string for the next stop and that's also weird because I didn't know Ben Y's stop is the same as my stop. And then she pulls my elbow in a way stronger way than I thought she could and she drags me off the bus even though I don't want to get off the bus and all of my concerns are leaking out of my eyes and some from my nose which is gross but Ben Y does not seem to care.

▫ ▫ ▫ ▫

It's a deep almost-all-the-way-night blue black outside and it should probably feel super weird that Ben Y's hand is still squeezing my elbow as we walk, but actually it feels warm and sturdy and way better than walking all by myself.

▫ ▫ ▫ ▫

How does Ben Y even know where I live?

▫ ▫ ▫ ▫

As soon as I open the door I see my sister Carolina in her pink leotard and she looks very, very *concerned* with wet cheeks and a pink nose and Mom rushes to me and grabs me in a hug and then Dad also hugs me and then Carolina climbs in the middle of us all and I don't ask about Spartacus because I guess I already know.

▫ ▫ ▫ ▫

The vet tech is standing in the doorway to the living room, the very same doorway I once ran into so hard that I grew a goose egg on my head just like in cartoons. Her mouth is not a serious shape anymore, it is a wide O shape and her eyes are just a little bit angry which confuses me because why would she be angry, but then Ben Y, who I forgot was here for a minute, says, *Mom?* and I'm so surprised to hear that, I almost don't see that behind the vet tech Spartacus is in the living room on her blanket on the couch. Spartacus who is not coughing, which is good, but who is not moving, which is bad. I almost don't see that. But I do.

▫ ▫ ▫ ▫

Can the vet tech fix *me* if my guts explode?

▫ ▫ ▫ ▫

Mom crushes my head to her chest and the whole family sits on the floor next to Spartacus who is on the couch, which is a backward situation if you think about it, and yes Spartacus is not alive anymore and this is the worst day of my whole life.

JAVIER

`<jajajavier:)>`

I COULDN'T SLEEP.
I MISSED PLAYING WITH EVERYONE.
IT WAS LATE. I SAW THE CHAT LOG

EVEN
JERK'S
THEY WERE
THOUGH

NO ONE AROUND

SLEEPY
TIME
TEA

WORLD'S
#5
MOM
MUG

OLD ARTS
NOTEBOOKS

MOM

B) FORGIVE AND FORGET?

Now WHAT?

A) STAY MAD?   C) PRETEND
                   NOTHING
                     HAPPENED?

D) NONE OF THE ABOVE?

BEN B

<BenBee>

The twitch of his eye,
a slight wiggle,
barely noticeable
(but I notice it)
as he reads the note
while Mom reads the
    newspaper,
while I eat my cereal.

He sips coffee,
grimacing
as it steams up his glasses.
He reads the note again.

Why now?

He says the words to himself,
and it's like I can see them
floating in front of us,
murmurs made of small fonts.

Um.

My voice is a bigger font,
bold,
no flourish,
standing tall,
even if the word
is a dumb one.

My teacher said
I'm one of the best typists
she's ever met.
She said if I type in class,
my notes and assignments
and tests,
it could help me . . .

I test out a new fancy word,
underlined in my brain:

excel.

Mom looks up from the
newspaper.
Dad frowns.

But . . .
a 504?
Really?
Now?
In the seventh grade?
You'd need . . . a diagnosis.
Doctors. Psychologists, maybe.
Why hasn't anyone mentioned
    this before?
Who is this teacher?
Why are you typing in a
    emedial reading class?

He sets the letter down,
stands,
pours more coffee,
cleans his glasses.

My fonts all fall away.
I don't have answers.
I've been thinking:
*finally something to help me
    do better,*
not *why now*
not *what's wrong.*

I think Ms. J is right.
My chin sticks out,
all by itself,
a stubborn protest
against the way Dad said
Who is this teacher?

I've tried it.
For a while now.
Typing in class.
It works.
For real.
It works great.
*And you always want me to
    be great, so . . .*

Dad sips his coffee,
curses under his breath,
at the boiling heat, or . . .

I don't know, kiddo.
A 504 . . .
that's new territory.
Territory for other kids,
special kids.
Not kids like you.

His font is bigger now,
his words snap snap snap,
clicking together.
Firm.

My words are lost,
swallowing by his bigger
meaning.

What did he just say?
About being special?

I don't have words
to figure that out.

▫ ▫ ▫ ▫

I mean,
any way my brain
repeats it:

. . . special kids.
Not kids like you.

It's not great.

Am I *not* special?
Is special *bad*?
Do I not *want* to be
    special, then?
I don't understand.

▫ ▫ ▫ ▫

Mom looks in the rearview
    mirror,
not at the cars behind us,
but at me,
in the backseat,
on the way to school.

Dad is only being cautious,
she says,
her gaze locking onto mine
while we idle
at a red light.

Remember the dyslexia fiasco?

I remember the test.
I remember no one had any
    answers.
I remember Dad just hired
    another tutor.
I remember Thursdays got
    doubled up,
and I couldn't eat dinner
until eight pm.
Is that what she means?

I catch her eyes in the mirror,
I shrug,
just before the light turns green,
just before she looks back at
    the road.

Sometimes I don't really
understand Dad,
I say quietly, almost under
    my breath.

Sometimes I don't either,
Mom says, even quieter
    than me.

▫ ▫ ▫ ▫

Dysfluency.

Ms. J typed that in the chat.
She meant Javier's stuttering.

Dysgraphia.

Ms. J wrote that in the letter
    for Mom and Dad.
She meant my awful
handwriting,
my note-taking,
my pencil grip.

Dyslexia.

A test I took years ago.
Inconclusive. Does this child
    have anxiety?

What is Ben Y's dys, I wonder.

What is Jordan J's dys?

Maybe the word for all of us
    should be

dysvergent.

▫ ▫ ▫ ▫

Or no, wait.

There's already a word.

Dysfunctional.

▫ ▫ ▫ ▫

It's like a bunch of whispers,
the willow branches
blowing around me
as I lie in the grass,
looking up,
blinded by the sun,
crushed by the heat.

What is it saying to me?
The tree?
I listen so so carefully.
I try to hear every tiny breath,
but it's all just out of reach,
like everything is for me,
so close,
but so far,
teasing me,
pretending I can hear it,
pretending I can get there,
pretending I'm good enough,

when the whispers already know
they aren't for me.
They're never for me.

□ □ □ □

I hear the bell.
Class has officially started.
I am still officially lying in
    the grass
under the tree.
I don't care if Mom saw me
dart under the fronds
instead of into the school
before she drove off.
I don't care
at
all.

Ben.

Ben B.

This time it's a real whisper,
I hear it clearly.
I sit up.

Sweat drips down my cheek,
tickling me,
as I peek
around the branches.

Javier.
Hoodie tied around his waist
    this time.
I can see his whole head
    and face
for the first time.

Buzz cut.
Big eyes.
Serious mouth.

Hi.

Hi.

You're late for class.

S-S-So are you.

BEN Y

<0benwhY>

I don't know why I came here.
It's not like Jordan J
is my bff,
but maybe
we're . . . something?
Friends with an asterisk?
Not bestie besties,
but not nothings.

Should I knock on the door?
Is he even here?
I should be in school.
He should be in school.

I bet on my eleventh toe
he's not in school.

I wouldn't be.
If I were him.

□ □ □ □

I see the asterisk
in his eyes
as he opens the front door
wider.

I feel the little starry spikes
hooking into me
like sticker burrs,
pulling me through the
    doorway,
into the house.

□ □ □ □

Not besties.
But not nothings.

□ □ □ □

[low and slow fart noise]

□ □ □ □

Can losing a dog possibly be
even sort of
kind of
sideways close
to losing a brother?

Can the pain
sear and pop
and burn and flame

the same way
every day
for weeks
and months
and . . .

for a full whole
entire
year?

Like it does?
Still?
Today?
THE day?

Can Jordan J
feel
even a little tiny bit
of what I feel?

Is that what friends with an
        asterisk
is all about?

Is that why I'm here?
Instead of anywhere else?

□ □ □ □

We sit on the floor,
not on the couch.

Jordan J's mom peeks in
        the room,
her curly hair tripping over
        itself,
falling to her shoulders,
like it's lost its way
either to
or from
her messy bun.

The TV is on.
Loud applause
fills the room.

Jordan J is quiet,
so quiet,
it confuses my ears.

It's the loudest, saddest quiet
I've ever heard.

JORDAN J

<JordanJmageddon!!!!>

Ben Y and I sit on the floor because Spartacus found her way to the Rainbow Bridge from the couch and even though Mom said the couch is fine and safe and just the same as it was before, which is probably true, I don't think I will ever sit on it again and I wish no one else would either and even though I can't feel happy right now, it almost makes me feel whatever happy might feel like when you're super sad that Ben Y just came right in and sat on the floor right next to me, no questions asked.

▫ ▫ ▫ ▫

I have fifty-three episodes of *Fierce Across America* recorded on my TV so that I can watch them any time I want which is pretty much all the time. *Ten dancers, ten choreographers, twenty lives changed. . . . This. Is. Fierce. Across. America.* I can do announcer Mae Michaelson's voice pretty much better than she can do her own voice even though she has a British accent and I have no accent though maybe I'd have an accent to her if she heard me talk. Do Florida people have accents? Maybe we sound like sweat and sunshine and sand and bare feet, but, like, all of that coming out of our mouths? I don't know, I just know that watching D'Andre pirouette right now is spinning a teeny teeny tiny bit of sadness away and maybe I should ask Ben Y why she's here except it feels like I know why even though I don't know why which is weird but I'm just going to go with it.

▫ ▫ ▫ ▫

It's a little bit weird that your mom sent my sweet Spartacus over the Rainbow Bridge last night. Those are the first words I say to Ben Y and I don't mean them in a mean way or anything just, it was weird and Ben Y looks at me like Mae Michaelson looks at Veronica Verve when Veronica says D'Andre's pirouettes could use a little work, which is to say, she looks at me like I am bananas bonkers. Then she says, Oh, you mean euthanized, but she trails off when she gets to the -ed part of the word because I guess she sees me make the ahhhhhh face I make when someone uses very specific and scary words about *la la la la la I don't want to think about it, any of it, nope nope nope nope nope,* and now I can't stop saying *nope* and rocking back and forth just a little bit while D'Andre gets schooled on not being too aggressive with his jetés, or as Mae Michaelson says, *Without better control, he risks injury to both himself and to the front row of the audience, hahahaha.* Am I also out of control enough to risk injury to myself and my audience, aka Ben Y, hahahaha? I want to stop rocking and saying nope, but I just can't yet.

▫ ▫ ▫ ▫

Ben Y says in a quiet voice that slides in between my nopes that her brother, her best friend, the only person in the world who understood her also died and how she knows that's not the same as a dog dying but it kind of is because her brain and her heart and her everything still hurt all the time when she misses him. She says maybe Spartacus will get to be dust in a box like her brother, which isn't as scary as it sounds because if you think about it, it's just like the dust that floats in space and eventually all collects together to make a planet, so basically her brother is in his post-human, pre-planet form right now and that idea is pretty freaking cool because can you imagine what a planet made out of Spartacus would be like? It would be an awesome planet full of love and snuggles and face licks and stinky farts. That makes me smile. Also dust is like sand and I like the idea of Spartacus being in her own sandbox.

□ □ □ □

I one hundred and fifty-five percent forgot that Mom was here, too, until she brings out a tub of ice cream and two spoons and puts it on the rug in front of me and Ben Y and winks and says, *Who's ready for second breakfast?*

□ □ □ □

Mom squeezes Ben Y's shoulder when she walks past us to go back to the kitchen to find some paper towels because I already accidentally dripped ice cream on the rug and Spartacus isn't here to lick it up. That makes it hard to swallow the ice cream that made it to my mouth because now my throat has a Spartacus-sized planet stuck in it and Ben Y sees my throat planet maybe, or maybe just has a brother-sized planet stuck in her own throat because she squeezes my shoulder like my mom squeezed hers, and it's like she squeezed out a smidge of sadness and replaced it with the warm feeling of *I got you*, just like D'Andre says *I got you* to Theresa when she leaps into his arms and he catches her tight and safe and spins her over his head while her smile goes from scared to relieved and you can see her body relax just a little and that's probably why Veronica Verve gave them ten out of ten, outstanding.

▫ ▫ ▫ ▫

I give Ben Y ten out of ten outstanding for that shoulder squeeze and for the way she can eat ice cream because dang there is already none left, get it girl. Then I ask her if she thinks pre-planet dust in a box can also be a little bit like being in your own Sandbox and maybe her brother is in his own Sandbox and would he think that was cool or no and she gives a tiny little cough as she swallows her ice cream and then she cries like really super hard and all I can do is cry a little bit with her because I always cry when other people cry and I point her face at my shoulder and pat her head like Mom patted my head last night until I fell asleep.

JAVIER

`<jajajavier:)>`

BEN B

<BenBee>

Javier puts his hoodie back on,
we grab our stuff,
and we are running.
I don't love running.
It's hot.
It's sweaty.
And yet
here we are.
Javier's long legs
cut through the tall grass
and I chase after him,
a panting puppy
running after a deer
or a gazelle
or what's that animal
with the twirly horns?
Kudu!
Javier is a kudu.
I am . . .
a corgi?

We run,
bursting through the
   school doors,
flying down the hallway,
stopping,
hands on our knees,

gasping,
sweat dripping,
so late,
trying to catch our breath
before we go through the
   last door,
into the stairwell,
to face the day.

▫ ▫ ▫ ▫

Her dress is golden today,
with black on its edges.
There are sun shapes,
shimmering on the fabric,
the same color,
but somehow they shine
even in the buzzing
ugly light
under the stairs.

Her dark eyes greet us.
Her mouth pressed in a line,
but not in a line I know.
It's thinner, tenser,
like maybe she's biting her lips
from the inside.

How kind of you boys,
she says,
to deign to come to class today.

Her voice is weird, too,
higher-pitched,
like it's almost joking,
but her face says
no way
no jokes
not now
sit down.

We sit down.

Ben B.
Can I have you at your
   desk today?

The computer in front of me
pings to life.

Turn that off,
and take your seat, please.

But . . .
I don't understand.
Is this because we were late?
Is she mad?
I thought I was the best typist
   in the world?
I thought this was our
   new plan?
My path to the 504?

For right now.
Please.
Your seat.

She points at my old desk.

And it's only now I realize
   two things.

One: Javier and I are the only
   kids here.

Two: There's a man I didn't
   see when we came in,
a man who could make better
choices about where to put
   his chair,

a man staring at us
like we are putting on a very
    interesting show
and no way is he moving
    his chair
because he has the best seat
in the house.

□ □ □ □

I don't suppose you two know
where everyone else is?

She tries to laugh,
a hairball noise,
a dry-throat noise,
a . . .
scared noise?

Javier and I shake our heads.
Ms. J blinks
and it takes so long
for her eyes to open,
I wonder if she's fallen asleep
standing up.

When her eyes open,
she breathes:

Wonderful.

A whisper so quiet,
under her breath,
I can barely hear it
even from my desk
right in front of her.

I can tell
she doesn't think anything
is wonderful
right now.

Well, let's go ahead
and get started.
The assessment retake
will be here before we know it.

Javier, can you remove your
    hoodie, please?
Dress code.

□ □ □ □

Not once
in all of the ten million days
we have been in summer school
has Ms. J ever
ever
asked Javier
to take off his hoodie.

He looks at me
instead of her.

I shrug.
He frowns.

And then—

□ □ □ □

A lot of things happen at once.

Jordan J and Ben Y
come smashing
through the door
running a hundred miles
    an hour.

The door crashes open
with such force

it slams into the man in
    the chair,
bouncing off him,
and then hitting him again
when it swings back.

He yelps,
grabs his nose,
his glasses skittering across
    the floor,
his notebook sliding off his lap,
a slap
as it lands at his feet.

Oh, shiiiiiiiiiiitake mushrooms!
Who's that guy?
Jordan J's voice bounces
    through the stairwell.

Ben Y starts to laugh,
a giggle at first,
then loud whoops,
then she seems to recognize
the bleeding guy,
then the whoops turn
    into gasps,
and then
she's crying

hard,
falling to her knees
right where she stands,
and
Ms. J crashes into her
on her way
to the man
whose nose is freely bleeding
down his chin
and onto his white
short-sleeved
button-up
shirt.

□ □ □ □

Uh.

□ □ □ □

Javier and I stay in our seats,
watching everything.

Tangles of arms and legs,
flashes of gold,
gushing nose blood,
and now Jordan J is crying, too,
on the floor, too,
hugging Ben Y

rocking back and forth
and what
is
even
happening.

□ □ □ □

Everyone is stunned quiet
except for the crying people.

Ms. J is back on her feet.
The man stands,
holding his bloody face with
        one hand,
his notebook with the other,
his glasses propped on his head
as if they were fancy sunglasses
and he was a superstar
who just got smashed in
        the face
with a basketball.
Or an elbow.

Or, you know,
a door.

□ □ □ □

Mr. Maillot.

Her voice is a shattered
    whisper.

Mr. Maillot,
as you can imagine, this—

He interrupts her
with a shaking,
rumbling
volcanic
erupting
voice:

I'll see you in the hallway,
Jordan.
Now.

Jordan looks up,
his face shining with tears.

I'm sorry. We didn't see
    you. We—

He means me.
Ms. J puts her hand on
    Jordan J's shoulder,
for just a second,
before she follows the man,
Mr. Maillot,
out the door.

She turns,
looks at us.

My name is Jordan, too.

BEN Y

<0BenwhY>

One year ago today.
Summer school.
At my desk.
Daydreaming.
Thinking about the potion.
Thinking I'd be a
     Ghostkiller now.
Wondering why Benicio
     taught me.
Wondering so many other
unimportant things
when
a man came in the classroom,
a man in a short-sleeved,
button-up
shirt,
a man named Mr. Maillot,
the vice principal,
a man who went to my teacher,
whispered in her ear,
and then kneeled by my desk,
asked me to please follow him
to the front office
which I did
and there was my mom
and Valentina
and Esme

faces blank
with shock
at school to pick me up
take me to the hospital.
There had been an accident—
Benicio's car
the rain
a curve,

and Mr. Maillot held my hand,
walked us to the car,
then

wished

us

luck.

▫ ▫ ▫ ▫

Mr. Maillot.
An angel of death.
Holding my hand
as I took my first steps,
my baby steps,
into a new world,
a foreign place,

a universe that somehow
   existed
without
my brother in it.

□ □ □ □

And it was like he really was
   some kind of angel,
because I never saw him again.

Maillot.

I didn't go back to summer
   school,
and he wasn't at school during
   the school year.

Gone, poof, like he'd been
   made of smoke.

□ □ □ □

But now he's here?
Bleeding in my classroom?
I can't . . .
I don't . . .

Who is he here for?
Who else has died?
Whose hand is he about
   to hold?
Please,
please,
please,
don't have it be mine again.
Please don't have it be
   anyone's.

JORDAN J

<JORDANJMAGEDDON!!!>

Wait wait wait wait wait wait wait wait wait wait wait wait.

▫ ▫ ▫ ▫

Ms. J is also Jordan J? There are two Jordan Js in this class?? How will anyone tell us apart???

▫ ▫ ▫ ▫

Is her middle name also nothing because she doesn't have one like I don't have one????????? Is this why she also does fart noises some-times????? Is this why we both get so many chat infractions??? Because those are all things Jordan Js do??????

▫ ▫ ▫ ▫

A lot of questions about a lot of things are flying around inside my head right now and also a lot of feelings are still inside me because of Spartacus and now this dude who is a stranger is bleeding all down his face in a super yucky way and that's because I hit him with the door, which was by accident. Except, wait, even though it was kind of a photo finish, I'm pretty sure Ben Y beat me in the race so tech-nically she hit him with the door and is that why she's sitting on the floor crying and crying and crying?

▫ ▫ ▫ ▫

It was Ben Y who said maybe we should stop eating ice cream and go to school, that maybe school would somehow make us feel better and maybe she needed to say she was sorry for yelling at Ms. J even though Ms. J totally deserved it and maybe it would be nice to see our friends and since Ms. J is learning how to farm pigs in Sandbox that will probably be funny to watch, all the pigs running around, so I said okay sure, let's go and Mom said, Are you two sure? And we said yes and she said, Okay, let's get in the car, and we said maybe we can walk? And she said it's really far, are you sure and we said sure and started walking.

□ □ □ □

It *was* really far, though, and also really hot so we decided to take the bus but the bus broke down which, what, that has never happened before and we had to wait for a new bus and so by the time we got to school we weren't just late we were really really really late and I was like, maybe we should run and Ben Y was like I'll beat you there and I was like, no way, and then! It! Was! A! Race!

□ □ □ □

And now we're here and maybe it wasn't such a good idea to come. Ben Y is crying and crying and we all know what's going to happen when I see someone crying and crying, just like when I see someone throwing up. So now we're both crying and crying (but at least not throwing up) and I know she's crying because of her brother and I'm crying because of Spartacus and we're hugging each other and crying but not in a weird way just in a sad way and I just heard that bleeding guy ask me to come out into the hallway but Ms. J said no, Jordan, he means me, and I really feel like this day has spiraled out of control.

JAVIER

`<JaJaJavier:)>`

BEN B

<BenBee>

We wait.
We wait.
We wait.
We wait.

Ms. J,
Mr. Maillot,
they don't come back.

We wait.
We wait.
We wait.
We wait.

The bell rings.

Should we stay?
Should we go?

No one says anything.
We keep sitting
until Javier stands,
and one, by one
shows us all
what he just drew.

Oh
shiiiiiiiitake mushrooms.

BEN Y

<0BenwhY>

He's right.
Javier is totally right.

This was Ms. J's assessment.
She told us it was coming.
This was her teacher FART.

Son of a bench.

JORDAN J

<JORDANJMAGEDDON!!!>

If Javier is right and he is very much probably right, then hopefully Ms. J will get to retake her teacher assessment FART like we all get to retake the regular FART, and hopefully she will pass like hopefully we all will pass and hopefully everything will be fine for everyone just like how in *Fierce Across America* they sometimes have a Save Your Bootie Dance when the judges give someone a low score but the audience thinks the dancer just had a bad day or whatever so the dancer dances really, really hard to save their bootie and to try to add points to their score. Ms. J has been working all summer to help us save our booties, so we can definitely make sure to help her save her own.

JAVIER

`<jajajavier:)>`

WHERE IS Ms. J?
WILL ANYTHING BE THE SAME AGAIN?!
WHAT WOULD SPARTACUS DO?

 CHAT

Divergent Dingleberries

Private server created by: **BenBee**

Password required

Avatar name:

Password:

Remember! Ghost Season is coming! Protect your lives, your health, and your gold by avoiding ghosts at all costs. Think you can outsmart the ghosts by logging out? Think again! All logged out avatars will remain in sleeping mode, so make sure you're protected. Get melted during Ghost Season? Gonna cost ya!

In order to bring you the very best game possible, Sandbox is moving to a pay-per-play model. Survive Ghost season? You'll maintain VIP status and continue on the free platform. Get melted? You can retrieve your gold and items when you sign up for one of our affordable monthly plans. Click here for more details.

JORDANJMAGEDDON!!!: OBenwhY, you okay?

OBenwhY: nah.
OBenwhY: you okay?

JORDANJMAGEDDON!!!: nah
JORDANJMAGEDDON!!!: but maybe we both will be okay some day

BenBee ENTERS GAME

BenBee: You guys okay?
BenBee: What happened in class today? all the crying stuff

OBenwhY: It's just a bad day for me.
OBenwhY: A really, really bad day.

JORDANJMAGEDDON!!!: Same.

BenBee: Yikes. Well, I hope you both feel better soon.

JORDANJMAGEDDON!!!: Me too.

OBenwhY: Me too.

jajajavier:) ENTERS GAME

jajajavier:): hey everyone

jajajavier:): do you think ms. j will find us?

jajajavier:): here, I mean?

jajajavier:): tonight?

jajajavier:): tell us what happened?

JORDANJMAGEDDON!!!: she found me before, after my Terrible Spartacus Idea

BenBee: she might. cause she's not like a regular teacher

JORDANJMAGEDDON!!!!: definitely not a teacher griefer.

BenBee: she's like a friend teacher or a teacher friend

BenBee: kind of

BenBee: i don't know

BenBee: there isn't a word for what she is

JORDANJMAGEDDON!!!: yes there is

BenBee: what

JORDANJMAGEDDON!!!: divergent

BenBee: haha

jajajavier:): haha

0BenwhY: omg

BenBee: you're right, though

BenBee: she's a divergent teacher

BenBee: she teaches differently

BenBee: she, like, listens to us.

0BenwhY: she listens to you

0BenwhY: i don't know if she ever listened to ME.
i don't know if she actually ever saw ME. It was
always Benita this, Benita th—

CHAT INFRACTION

0BenwhY: GAH! it's like she seemed maybe soft and
nice and cool and different, but was she?

JORDANJMAGEDDON!!!: wait. she's not DEAD, is she?

0BenwhY: omg Jordan j, no she's not dead, she's like,
a real-life griefer.

0BenwhY: super extra annoying, though there *was* that
nice part trying to emerge, just, can you be nice AND
clueless—

CHAT INFRACTION

BenBee: Ben Y! You're about to get ejected.

jajajavier:): You can totally be nice and clueless.
Like Jordan J.

JORDANJMAGEDDON!!!: Hey!

JORDANJMAGEDDON!!!: I resemble that remark.

BenBee: seriously tho, you guys

BenBee: I mean, you y'alls, why didn't Ms. J come back to class today?

OBenwhY: we can ask her tomorrow

OBenwhY: she'll tell us if she wants to

OBenwhY: or if she thinks it will make Javier read out loud finally

OBenwhY: 😜

JORDANJMAGEDDON!!!: 😱

JORDANJMAGEDDON!!!: I'm really sorry, btw

JORDANJMAGEDDON!!!: about the reading thing

JORDANJMAGEDDON!!!: I just wanted to help

JORDANJMAGEDDON!!!: you're definitely right that people can be nice AND clueless

JORDANJMAGEDDON!!!: I will work very hard to have a clue now

JORDANJMAGEDDON!!!: and still be nice

JORDANJMAGEDDON!!!: sorrysorrysorrysorry

jajajavier:): eventually, i figured out you y'alls weren't making fun of me.

jajajavier:): but it still felt like it, with the finishing of my words and yelling my name

JORDANJMAGEDDON!!!: i'm really ten times sorry.

OBenwhY: we all are.

BenBee: infinity sorry.

jajajavier:): fine. I guess I forgive you, nerds. You all get an extra life as my friend.

JORDANJMAGEDDON!!!: do you think Ms. J will get an extra life?
JORDANJMAGEDDON!!!: for the teacher FART that we probably made her fail?

BenBee: dunno. for some reason this kind of feels like it WAS her extra life.

JORDANJMAGEDDON!!!: uh oh

jajajavier:): uh oh

BenBee: uh oh

OBenwhY: uh oh

BEN B

<BenBee>

Mr. Maillot greets us,
from behind Ms. J's desk.
She is definitely not here.
He is definitely not smiling.

The bandage on his nose
is so white,
it glows
under the buzzing lights.

Black half circles
spread under his eyes
like he's the one, when
after a fight,
someone says,
You should see the other guy.

Those are
definitely
other guy
eyes.

BEN Y

<0BenwhY>

His voice is so low,
I lean forward
to hear him,
even though
that's dumb
and doesn't help.

He says Ms. J is away
and my stomach fills
    with flames.
My mouth shouts,

Away for how long?
Just today?
Or . . . ?

He doesn't answer me.
Instead—
and this,
this
is when the flames in my belly
turn to burning acid:
he puts a copy of Oliver Twist
on every desk
and says,

Your reading assignment
    has changed.
Please turn to the preface
    so that we can begin.
We have some catching up
    to do,
if we're to finish the book
    before
you retake the assessment.

He looks down at a sheet
    of paper on the desk,
looks up,
says,

Benita Ybarra,
please begin reading.

And, yeah,

his brain?
It's full of shiitake mushrooms,

if he thinks
for one second
I'm reading this

instead of
the end of
Save Ur Server, Save Urself.

I mean,
we're almost done!
Are we going to save the server
and ourselves
or what?!

I'm pretty sure Oliver Twist
can't answer that question.
Only we can.

▫ ▫ ▫ ▫

And it's Ben Y,
you dink.

JORDAN J

<JORDANJMAGEDDON!!!>

First of all, we are so close to being finished with Save *Ur Server, Save Urself* by Tennessee Williamson, there is no way in a million years I'm going to start reading a new book. I mean come on I have never finished reading a book ever and now that we're at the end he's going to take it away and make us start over again on some old book with 9893673547 pages and words that are so tiny they dance like fleas???? That is just more nopes than I can nope right now and I have been noping A LOT lately.

□ □ □ □

Second of all, where in the world is Ms. J (no relation, but exact same name!). Maybe she's mad at us for messing up her teacher FART or maybe she's sad that she probably failed it or maybe she has the stomach flu which can really knock you out trust me I know, or duh duh duh duh, of course! She's probably watching back-to-back episodes of *Fierce Across America* and eating ice cream until she feels better because that is what I do when I'm sad or mad and of course that's what she's doing because we are both Jordan Js which makes us the same even though there's no relation.

□ □ □ □

I wish I was eating ice cream and watching *Fierce Across America* right now.

□ □ □ □

[fart noise]

JAVIER

`<jajajavier:)>`

IF YOU CHOOSE TO READ
SAVE UR SERVER, SAVE URSELF
SO THAT YOU CAN SAY YOU
FINALLY READ A BOOK FROM
BEGINNING TO END, THEN
FIND MS. J

IF YOU CHOOSE TO STOP NOW
AND READ Oliver Twist, THEN

NO WAY, NO ONE WOULD
EVER

Maybe we should Spartacus Ms J ! Let's watch the movie

CHOOSE THAT

but how would that help?

uh-oh! Maillot is coming! Javier! Hide your notebook!

mehWhere's my

BEN B

<BenBee>

She's not in class.
Again.

It's been days.
And days.
And days.
No typing.
No Sandbox.
*No Save Ur Server, Save
   Urself.*
Only stupid *Oliver Twist*
and stupid

Mr. Maillot
and everything is stupid
and UGH.

It's not possible that we got
   her *fired,*
right?

It's not possible that she's never
   coming back,
right?

BEN Y

<0BenwhY>

My book flushing,
my book choice,
the two of us taking the
computers,
my yelling at her,
my crashing through the door,
my smashing Maillot's nose,
my tripping her
as I collapsed,
crying with Jordan J . . .

Is Ms. J gone
because she finally had
    enough?

Is all of this
Oliver Twist torture,
and no Sandbox,

and Maillot's
blah blah blah-ing
technically
and
officially
my fault?

Did Ms. J get fired?
Because of *me?*

Or worse,
Did she *quit?*
Because of me?

JORDAN J

<JORDANJMAGEDDON ! ! !>

I'm just saying, if Ms. J (same name, no relation) is still eating ice cream and watching *Fierce Across America* we might need to have an intervention or something because it has been a lot of days and my mom always says *you can't just sit in front of the TV, Jordan, you have to feel the sunshine on your face,* and where is Ms. J's face in relation to the sunshine today, that's what I'm wondering while I'm trying not to wonder if we got her fired and might never see her again.

□ □ □ □

I'm also wondering if Mr. Maillot could make this class any more boring not that that's a challenge it's just that Ms. J managed to teach us all the same things in a non-boring way so now we know that it's possible and knowing that it's possible to learn things in fun and divergent ways makes Mr. Maillot's boringness even worse, you know, like he's trying on purpose to make everything terrible or maybe he's just clueless like I was which I guess is fine because it can be fixed but also he just said the FART retake is next Monday and I'm not super great at math but even I know that if you add being terrible plus being mostly clueless plus the FART retake next Monday, then that equals please please Ms. J get back here as fast as you can.

JAVIER

`<jajajavier:)>`

EVERYTHING IS FALLING APART, BUT...
IT ALSO FEELS, WEIRDLY, LIKE EVERYTHING
IS COMING TOGETHER. I THINK,... I THINK I FINALLY
HAVE FRIENDS

BEN B

<BenBee>

She said it was okay.
She said the accommodation is
    in my file.
She said there's a FART retake
designed for the computer,
for kids like me,
to type our answers,
to make things more equal. . . .

My voice wobbles
more than I want it to,
but I don't move
from this spot,
from my computer.
I keep standing,
just like Spartacus did
in the movie Jordan J made
    us watch,
and he was right,
it was pretty good,
and Spartacus was pretty brave,
and maybe I can be brave, too.
Mr. Maillot points to my desk.
My old desk.

The one he's made me sit in
since Ms. J disappeared.

Ms. Jackson was unable to
    arrange the
teacher discretion
accommodation
before . . . before I arrived,
and if you are not in the
    504 system,
I am unable to help you.
Please take your seat.

I hear the words
coming out of his mouth,
my stomach flip-flops.

Then I hear the words
coming out of my mouth:

Ms. J . . .
she would never, ever
not have arranged the 504
unless . . .
unless . . .

I glance at Ben Y,
at Jordan J,
at Javier,
their faces look scrambled,
like my flip-flopping guts.

Unless . . .
Is she in trouble?
She didn't . . .
she didn't get fired did she?

I mean, we had a deal,
Ms. J and I.
And I know now,
she doesn't go back
on her deals.

She would never do that.
Unless . . .

BEN Y

<0BenwhY>

I watch Ben B,
refusing to move,
standing his ground,
just like Spartacus
in the movie Jordan J made
   us watch,
in his living room,
eating cheese puffs,
like we were all
friends friends
and not just friends
with an asterisk.

Ben B is calm,
he's telling the truth,
he wants answers.

I do, too.
We all do.

I look down at the sheet
on my desk,
all the bubbles,
all the answers
empty,
unguessed.

Florida Rigorous Academic Assessment Test

We all worked so hard
preparing for this day.
And Ms. J,
maybe she worked the hardest
of us all
and no way
no way
would she miss this day,
unless . . .

Where is Ms. J?
Like, actually?
Where?
Why isn't she here?

My voice echoes Ben B's
   questions,
and it's loud,
louder than I expected.
Almost as loud
as when I yelled at Ms. J,
when I was burning,
flaming mad at her,
and it doesn't even matter

if I'm still mad at her
because everything that's
    happening
today,
yesterday,
all these days with Maillot . . .
something isn't right.
Something is definitely,
definitely
wrong.

My voice gets even louder:
Did she really get fired?
For what?

I stand up.
I shake the test at him.

You don't get answers,
until we get answers.

Mr. Maillot scrunches his face,
folding his lips and nose
into such a sharp point
he could maybe use it
to dig a tunnel
through the wall,
escaping all of us
and our questions.

Sit down.

His voice is loud, too.
His pointy face narrows
    even more.

SIT DOWN.

And that's when everyone else
stands up.

JORDAN J

<JORDANJMAGEDDON!!!>

I feel like I might have to make a not-good choice in a minute because this Maillot guy is telling Ben B to move away from the computers and sit at his desk so we can start the testing on time and Ben Y is asking where the heck Ms. J (same name!) (no relation) is because it has been a LOT of days since we saw her and she would have to be melted by a ghost or abducted by aliens to miss the actual FART re-take day that we've all been planning for for a million weeks, except Ben Y doesn't say melted by a ghost or abducted by aliens, she says *fired* and that fills my brain with more wrinkles than a dress shirt you find wadded up and lost under the re-usable grocery bags in the trunk of your mom's car. *Fired?* Oh man, oh man.

▫ ▫ ▫ ▫

Now we're *all* standing because mean-voiced Maillot shouted at Ben Y and Ben B to sit down and then Javier says out loud in his own deep voice *B-B-B-Ben B already has acc-acco-mo-mo-modations and th-th-that's as g-g-good as a 504 unless y-y-you wa-wa-want to be a di-di-dink about it* and the guy says *QUIET* and I bet that's the first time ever in the history of everything that anyone has ever told Javier to be quiet.

▫ ▫ ▫ ▫

Everyone is standing and I think maybe we are Spartacusing without even realizing we're doing it!

Javier yanks his answer sheet off of his desk and holds it up so we can all see it and what there is no way he could be finished by now because we don't even have the question booklet yet and I squint so I can see Javier's amazing ESP answers and wow wow YES, we *are* totally Spartacusing in sync and I knew they were going to like that movie and oh man Javier is going to fail the FART but it will be so worth it. He grabs his stuff, drops the answer sheet on Mr. Maillot's desk that is really Ms. J's desk that is really a table, and he walks out of the classroom.

▫ ▫ ▫ ▫

It doesn't take long for the rest of us to follow Javier's lead and drop our answer sheets on Mr. Maillot's desk that is really Ms. J's desk that is really a table, and I know that this whole thing that is happening right now is probably medium important to the whole big world, but it feels very, very important to our world under the stairs, and I hope our parents realize that when we all fail the FART re-take with, like, big goose egg zeroes.

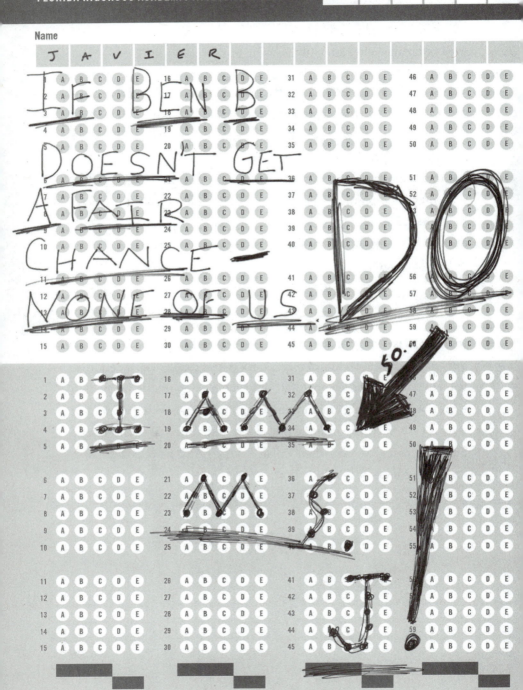

Name

B E N   B

1	A B C D E	16	A B C D E	31	A B C D E	46	A B C D E
2	A B C D E	17	A B C D E	32	A B C D E	47	A B C D E
3	A B C D E	18	A B C D E	33	A B C D E	48	A B C D E
4	A B C D E	19	A B C D E	34	A B C D E	49	A B C D E
5	A B C D E	20	A B C D E	35	A B C D E	50	A B C D E
6	A B C D E	21	A B C D E	36	A B C D E	51	A B C D E
7	A B C D E	22	A B C D E	37	A B C D E	52	A B C D E
8	A B C D E	23	A B C D E	38	A B C D E	53	A B C D E
9	A B C D E	24	A B C D E	39	A B C D E	54	A B C D E
10	A B C D E	25	A B C D E	40	A B C D E	55	A B C D E
11	A B C D E	26	A B C D E	41	A B C D E	56	A B C D E
12	A B C D E	27	A B C D E	42	A B C D E	57	A B C D E
13	A B C D E	28	A B C D E	43	A B C D E	58	A B C D E
14	A B C D E	29	A B C D E	44	A B C D E	59	A B C D E
15	A B C D E	30	A B C D E	45	A B C D E	60	A B C D E

I am nice and cool and awesome and not mean.

I listen to people.

1	A B C D E	16	A B C D E	31	A B C D E	46	A B C D E
2	A B C D E	17	A B C D E	32	A B C D E	47	A B C D E
3	A B C D E	18	A B C D E	33	A B C D E	48	A B C D E
4	A B C D E	19	A B C D E	34	A B C D E	49	A B C D E
5	A B C D E	20	A B C D E	35	A B C D E	50	A B C D E
6	A B C D E	21	A B C D E	36	A B C D E	51	A B C D E
7	A B C D E	22	A B C D E	37	A B C D E	52	A B C D E
8	A B C D E	23	A B C D E	38	A B C D E	53	A B C D E
9	A B C D E	24	A B C D E	39	A B C D E	54	A B C D E
10	A B C D E	25	A B C D E	40	A B C D E	55	A B C D E
11	A B C D E	26	A B C D E	41	A B C D E	56	A B C D E
12	A B C D E	27	A B C D E	42	A B C D E	57	A B C D E
13	A B C D E	28	A B C D E	43	A B C D E	58	A B C D E
14	A B C D E	29	A B C D E	44	A B C D E	59	A B C D E
15	A B C D E	30	A B C D E	45	A B C D E	60	A B C D E

I AM AMAZING

You are not even close

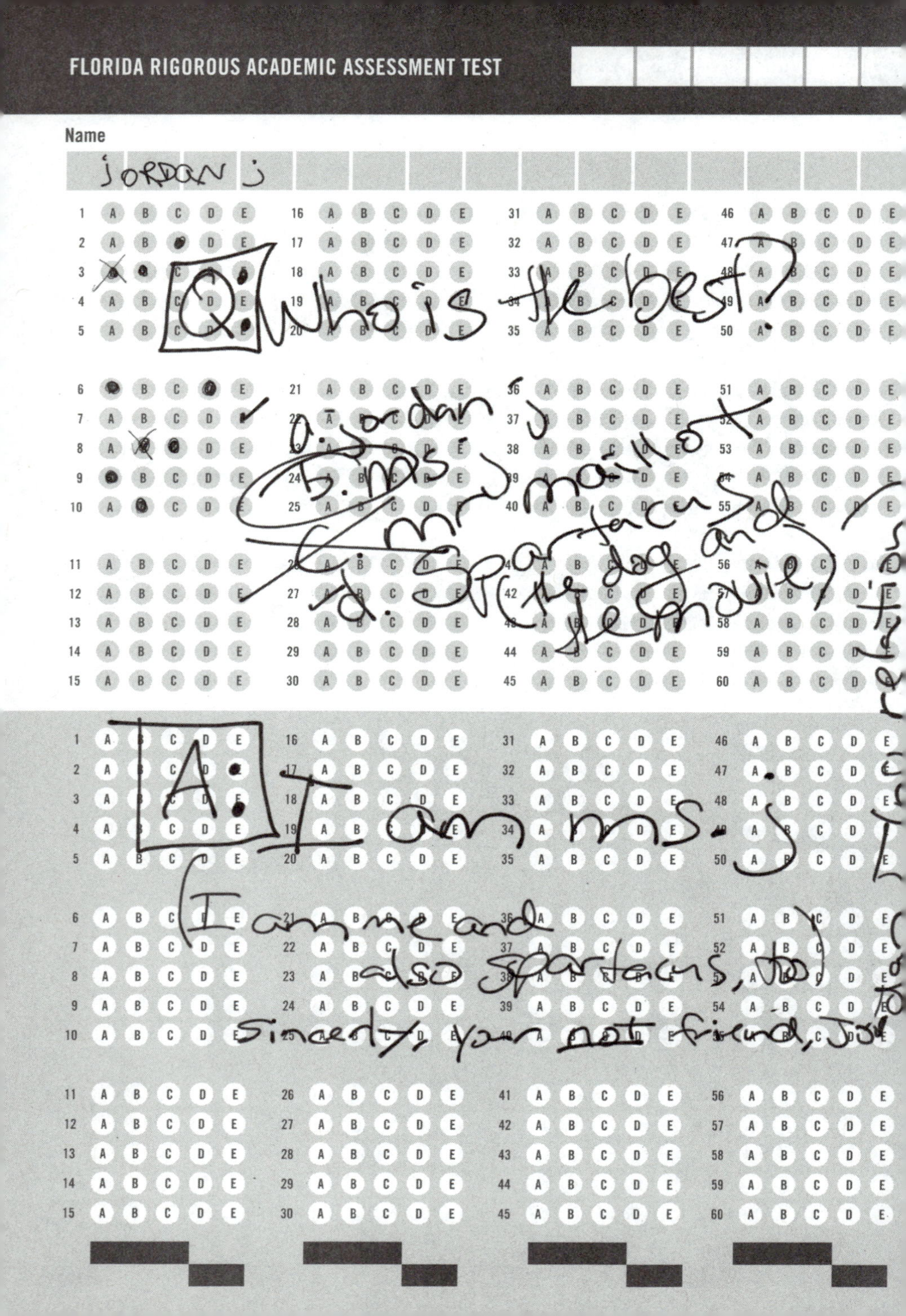
FLORIDA RIGOROUS ACADEMIC ASSESSMENT TEST
Name
JORDAN J
Q. Who is the best?
a. Jordan J
b. Ms. J
c. Mr. Maillot
d. Spartacus (the dog and the movie)
A. I am Ms. J
(I am me and also Spartacus, too)
Sincerely, your not friend, J.J.

Name

B e n   Y

this ↓
does
not
matter

U know what matters? →

being kind and Q safe even if U R clueless.

I am (trying to b like) MS J.

R U kind and safe? like ms. j. →

No U R not

1 A B C D E   16 A B C D E   31 A B C D E   46 A B C D E
2 A B C D E   17 A B C D E   32 A B C D E   47 A B C D E
3 A B C D E   18 A B C D E   33 A B C D E   48 A B C D E
4 A B C D E   19 A B C D E   34 A B C D E   49 A B C D E
5 A B C D E   20 A B C D E   35 A B C D E   50 A B C D E
6 A B C D E   21 A B C D E   36 A B C D E   51 A B C D E
7 A B C D E   22 A B C D E   37 A B C D E   52 A B C D E
8 A B C D E   23 A B C D E   38 A B C D E   53 A B C D E
9 A B C D E   24 A B C D E   39 A B C D E   54 A B C D E
10 A B C D E   25 A B C D E   40 A B C D E   55 A B C D E
11 A B C D E   26 A B C D E   41 A B C D E   56 A B C D E
12 A B C D E   27 A B C D E   42 A B C D E   57 A B C D E
13 A B C D E   28 A B C D E   43 A B C D E   58 A B C D E
14 A B C D E   29 A B C D E   44 A B C D E   59 A B C D E
15 A B C D E   30 A B C D E   45 A B C D E   60 A B C D E

1 A B C D E   16 A B C D E   31 A B C D E   46 A B C D E
2 A B C D E   17 A B C D E   32 A B C D E   47 A B C D E
3 A B C D E   18 A B C D E   33 A B C D E   48 A B C D E
4 A B C D E   19 A B C D E   34 A B C D E   49 A B C D E
5 A B C D E   20 A B C D E   35 A B C D E   50 A B C D E
6 A B C D E   21 A B C D E   36 A B C D E   51 A B C D E
7 A B C D E   22 A B C D E   37 A B C D E   52 A B C D E
8 A B C D E   23 A B C D E   38 A B C D E   53 A B C D E
9 A B C D E   24 A B C D E   39 A B C D E   54 A B C D E
10 A B C D E   25 A B C D E   40 A B C D E   55 A B C D E
11 A B C D E   26 A B C D E   41 A B C D E   56 A B C D E
12 A B C D E   27 A B C D E   42 A B C D E   57 A B C D E
13 A B C D E   28 A B C D E   43 A B C D E   58 A B C D E
14 A B C D E   29 A B C D E   44 A B C D E   59 A B C D E
15 A B C D E   30 A B C D E   45 A B C D E   60 A B C D E

BEN B

<Benbee>

Dad's mouth hangs open.
I can see the bite of chicken
still in there,
floating in space.

Mom's wine glass is paused,
halfway to her mouth,
which is also open
just a little bit.

Say that again?
Mom sets her wine glass down.

I say it again.

Dad swallows his chicken bite,
coughs for a second, says,
You realize this means
all these weeks,
all these early mornings,
summer school itself,
in its entirety,
was a waste.

Mom looks at me,
really looks at me,
in my eyes,
from across the table.

That sounds like quite a day.

I smile.
She smiles.
Dad frowns,
pushes his seat from the table,
stomps away,
muttering,
Such a waste.

It doesn't feel like a waste,
    though.
Who cares about the s
    tupid FART.
Right now I only care about
    one thing:
finding Ms. J
and making her
our divergent teacher
again.

▫ ▫ ▫ ▫

Hello?
Yes.
He's right here.
Whom may I say is calling?

*Mmm-hmm, what's your real
    name, kiddo?*
I'm not sure I believe you.
Hold on one second.

Mom mutes the phone.

*Do you have a friend named
    Jordan?*
Jordan Jackson?
Just like your teacher?

I laugh and nod.

Mom's cheeks turn bright pink.

Hello, Jordan?
I apologize.
It's just . . . very odd, isn't it?
Yes.
He's right here.

I'm still laughing
when I take the phone,
and say,
*What's up Jordan J
    No Relation?*

CHAT

Divergent Dingleberries

Private server created by: **BenBee**

Password required

Avatar name:

Password:

GHOST SEASON IS HERE!!!

GHOST SEASON IS HERE!!!

GHOST SEASON IS HERE!!!

GHOST SEASON IS HERE!!!

GHOST SEASON IS HERE!!!

GHOST SEASON IS HERE!!!

GHOST SEASON IS HERE!!!

JJ11347: Hello?

JJ11347: No one is here?

JJ11347: where ARE you all?? Ghost Season starts NOW.

JJ11347: I just read an article about a bug in the Ghost Season software and I'm very worried. We haven't finished the pyramid and

CHAT INFRACTION

JJ11347: ahhhh! The bug is erasing everyone's extra lives, their gold. Entire avatars are being DELETED. They're trying to

CHAT INFRACTION

JJ11347: ARRGGH. They're going to release an update to the update.

JJ11347: But if you get melted before the update you'll lose everything.

JJ11347: instead of building a pen for pigs I've built a pen for your avatars

JJ11347: i will keep you safe until you log on

JJ11347: but also i have to eat dinner

JJ11347: IRL

JJ11347: and i have a very important meeting in the morning

JJ11347: oh shoot no one is here to give me a pork chop

JJ11347: in the game I mean

JJ11347: i have pasta IRL

JJ11347: oh shiitake mushrooms, I'm going to have
to kill a pig and eat a pork chop

JJ11347: ok ok ok i can do it

JJ11347: and i can keep everyone safe until they show up

JJ11347: i'm a fierce pork chop eating warrior

JJ11347: wow this ghost-killing potion is quite useful

BEN Y

<0BenwhY>

The candle flickers,
almost going out,
then the flame reaches
high,
higher,
higher still,
almost as tall as the picture,
the one with Benicio
    holding me
the day I was born
and the smile on his little-
    boy face
is brighter than any candle
could ever be.

How are you?
How did the retake go today?

Mom rests her chin on my
    shoulder
as we both watch the flame
stretching tall.

And I keep meaning to ask,
how is your friend?
The one who lost his dog?

Sometimes not great.
Sometimes okay.
My answers work for all
    her questions.

Tell him I've been praying
    for him.
His whole family.
She gives my neck a peck,
a gentle kiss,
takes a step back.

I've been praying for you, too,
    Benita.
Esme and I,
every night,
before she goes to sleep.

Praying for me, why?
My voice is a whisper.
I don't want to accidentally
extinguish the flame.

For you to be happy, mija.
For you to love yourself.
For you to come back to us.

Benicio is gone,
but you are still here.
We pray for you to see that.
We pray for you to see that
      we see you.
You are loved.

But . . .
it's not Benita,
I say,
turning to face her.
If you really see me,
then you have to see that.
It's Ben.
I'm Ben now.
Not . . . not like I'm a boy,
just . . . I'm figuring it out,
who I am,
what I want,
what I like,
who I like,
all the things.
And I don't really know
      anything

about anything
yet . . .
except . . .
I'm not Benita,
not anymore.

Mom cups her hand on
      my cheek.

I love you
whoever you are
and whoever you become,
you understand me?

I nod.
The flame jumps high,
sputters low.

See?
He loves you, too, mija.
a tear slips down Mom's face,
as she nods at the candle, smiles.
He loves you, too.

▫ ▫ ▫ ▫

The phone never rings,
but it rings right now,
making Mom and I jump,
and for one tiny smidge of
    a second
I wonder if
maybe Benicio . . .
maybe he's calling to say hi
from the Great Beyond
or wherever he is.

Hello?

The words come at me fast,
just like they do on the bus,
not Benicio,
but that's okay.
Jordan J's voice,
comforting
in its noise.

I interrupt him to say,
I don't know.
Let me ask.

Then,
She says it's okay.
She's been praying for you,
and me, apparently.

I'll tell her.
And . . . you can tell everyone
I'm on my way.

JORDAN J

<JORDANJMAGEDDON!!!>

The cool thing about having a mom who is a smart person is that she can find cool things that she thinks you might want or need or like and so after I told her all about this bonkers day and failing the FART on purpose but for REASONS and how we're all worried Ms. J might have gotten fired because of us but we don't know what to do about it or even where she is, Mom got on the phone and she called the school but no one was there because it's late and then she called some other people and did her reporter work like she does for the newspaper and then she told me that Ms. J was suspended (teachers can get suspended??) and that she's having a meeting at school tomorrow to try to get unsuspended and I was like, *holy cats can we go to the meeting?* and Mom was like, *you can always try* and then she went upstairs and I could hear the printer printing and she came back downstairs with a bunch of sheets of paper and she handed them to me and said *maybe you could call your friends to come over and you could all fill these out. Bring them to your principal tomorrow morning, tell her what you told me, and cross all your fingers and toes.*

□ □ □ □

Oooh. Ooh. We'll have extra luck, too, because Ben Y has extra toes!

□ □ □ □

And so that's why it's kind of late at night but everyone is here in the living room with me at my house and no one is sitting on the sofa because I told them that's still Spartacus's place for a little bit and nobody minds because everyone is my friend and it's really cool to have all these friends right here on the floor with me. It is actually making me feel like the living room isn't such a sad place like I thought but is an okay place even if it was Spartacus's last place.

▫ ▫ ▫ ▫

We have the forms Mom printed and we have pens and markers and sodas and cheesy puffs and *Fierce Across America* is on in the background because it's always a good noise to have in your brain when you want to be smart or funny or brave or fierce or basically anything that is a little bit bigger than you, and we are laughing and writing and we are making a plan for tomorrow.

REAL-LIFE CHAT

Created by **everyone**

> **Avatar:** actual human bodies in Jordan J's actual living room (but not on the couch)

> **Password:** any words spoken out loud using actual mouths and voices

Typed up by Ben B

(just because it's always nice to have a chat log when you need to remember stuff)

Ben B: I can't believe my mom let me come over. It's dark outside and a school night and it's not, like, a 911 handwriting emergency or anything.

Ben Y: Have you ever had to leave the house at night for a 911 handwriting emergency?

Ben B: No. I never get to go anywhere at night, unless it's a soccer game or tutoring or something.

Ben Y: That is a bummer, man.

Ben B: Tell me about it.

Ben Y: I guess your mom could tell this is a teacher-saving emergency. Even parents understand that.

Javier: My m-m-mom was so excited that s-s-someone my own age actually called m-m-me on the phone, I think s-s-she would have let me f-f-fly to Mars.

Jordan J: It was super fun calling everyone on the phone, like, I forgot phones can even be used for calling! I liked to hear your voices instead of just seeing emojis or whatever and now I'm liking that your actual faces are in my house.

Ben Y: So now that we're all here, what's the plan?

Ben B: We have to finish building the pyramid! Haha. Just kidding. But wouldn't it be cool if we had a real-life pyramid made of diamonds that we could hide Ms J in?

Jordan J: That would be super cool. Except how would we get all those diamonds? They're very tiny in real life and Ms J is pretty regular-sized, so—

Ben Y: This is a fascinating conversation, you two, but we need a real plan. For real life.

Javier: Hey, uh, Jordan J's m-m-mom? Can you tell us exactly what you f-f-found out earlier?

Jordan J's Mom: Sure. Basically, there's going to be a meeting tomorrow to discuss why Ms. J was suspended and whether that warrants termination.

Jordan J: HOLY SHIITAKE MUSHROOMS! THEY'RE GOING TO KILL HER BECAUSE OF US?

Jordan J's Mom: Jordan. Baby. Relax. Termination means fire.

Jordan J: . . . .

Jordan J's Mom: *fired*. Like losing your job. Not the hot stuff.

Jordan J: Ooooooh. I get it. Right. So she has to dance for her life tomorrow. And maybe we can all somehow dance for her life with her.

Jordan J's Mom: . . .

Jordan J: Like in *Fierce Across America*? Mom! Come on! You've watched that show a thousand times with me, don't tell me you've never paid attention enough to realize that when someone gets almost voted off the show sometimes they have a chance to dance for their life so they can stay in the competition? What, Ben B, you don't have to raise your hand, this isn't class.

Ben B: Sorry. I just . . . it's already getting late and even though my mom was cool to let me come over, she's probably sitting in her car at the corner ready to come back and get me in, like, thirty minutes. We should probably get started figuring out a plan.

Ben Y: That's what *I've* been saying!

Javier: W-w-why don't w-w-we brainstorm some ideas? Grab some pens. We can use my notebook.

EVERYONE

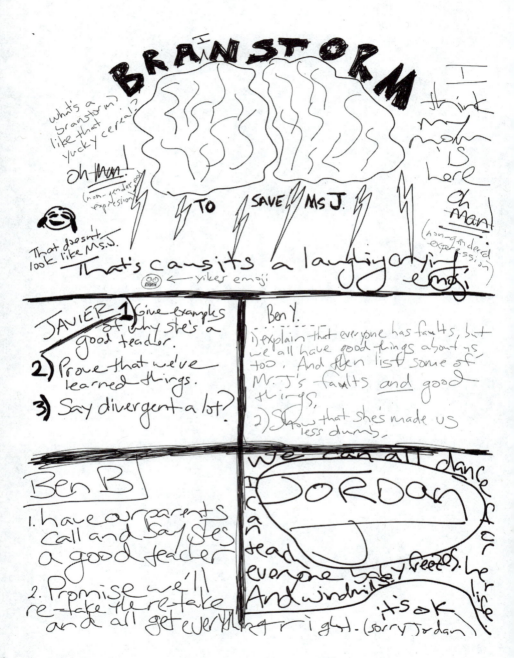

BRAINSTORM

what's a branstorm? like that yucky cereal?

I think mom is here

oh man! (non-gender-ed expression)

TO SAVE MS J.

Oh man! (non-gender-ed expression)

That doesn't look like Ms. J.

That's cause its a laughing crying emoji

← yikes emoji

JAVIER 1) Give examples of why she's a good teacher.

2) Prove that we've learned things.

3) Say divergent a lot?

Ben Y.

1) explain that everyone has faults, but we all have good things about us too. And then list some of Mr. J's faults and good things.

2) Show that she's made us less dumb.

Ben B

1. have our parents call and say she's a good teacher

2. Promise we'll re-take the re-take and all get everything right. (sorry Jordan)

We can all dance for JORDAN a teacher everyone baby needs. Her life. And windmills. it's ok

Can I call you y'all's again sometime?
i like remembering phones are for talking
sure!   OK!   Fine by me.

I

BRA^NSTOR
gah!

AFTER
A
SNACK...

M
I
I

how many sodas
have you had tonight?

A LOT!!!!!

you didn't draw
your mask.

I guess I'm as much
not hiding janymore?

What ever is   it's hard to
                             draw me!
Lot mask anyway?
                             electric
It's a luchador mask.   boogaloo
Look them up. They're awesome.
let's figure out how to Save Ms. J first, though, okay?

Save our server, save
herself.
hold on! Ben B yes! We have to help her help her self, like
she did with his!

Like make her read out loud?
Or we read out loud? TO
Show Javier's 1+2 & Beny's 2+
my, uh none of my ideas actually.
baby freeze \\ ..

BEN B

<Benbee>

We all squeeze into the
    front office.
Prepped.
Ready.

□ □ □ □

Jordan J.
Javier.
Ben Y.
Ben B.

Summer school.
Language Arts.
My class.
My friends.

The bell rings.
We are still in the front office.
The principal is in a meeting,
but not the Ms. J meeting.

We look back and forth
from one
to the other
to the other.

Ms. J is nowhere to be seen.

What now?

□ □ □ □

After her meeting,
the principal asks us to go
    to class.
We say no thank you.
She asks again.
We say no thank you.
She says she will come
    and get us
if Ms. J shows up,
but at this point
she is very
very
late
and so . . .

The principal crosses her arms.
She frowns.
She looks at the clock.
She says,

Class.
NOW.

No one moves.

□ □ □ □

The principal is on her
    computer,
looking up contact information
for all of our parents
when Ms. J rushes in,
her dress flying out around her,
her hair loose,
a cloud of curls.

There you are!
she shouts at us
Where have you been?
Do you have any idea what's
    been happening?

She's out of breath,
eyes a little wild,
and we all
all
start talking at once.

We've been here!
    Where have YOU been?
Did you get fired?
    We're trying to save you!
    Or, your job, really.
We're sorry we ruined your
assessment.
    We're here to fix it.
Or at least to try.

Our words fly,
a loud swarm
she shouts over:

I'VE BEEN SAVING YOU!
GHOST SEASON, Y'ALL!
HAVE YOU NOT HEARD
ABOUT THE BUG?
I'VE BEEN AWAKE
    ALL NIGHT.
ALL NIGHT!
The software just updated,
so you're all fine now,
but holy shirtballs,
y'all,
it was close for a while there,
but you're all fine now.

Did I already say that?
You're all fine.
Everyone is okay.
No one got erased.
Not under my watch.

She collapses into a chair.

It's hard to tell who is more
    surprised,
all of us,
or the principal,
whose mouth opens and
    closes twice
without any sound
at all.

BEN Y

<0BenwhY>

We thought we were
   saving her,

but she was saving us.
In the game,
and now here,
in the principal's office,
explaining everything.
Sandbox,
the reading out loud,
the Very Bad Day,
all of it.

▫ ▫ ▫ ▫

Ben B flicks on his phone,
we all look down
and
whoa
whoa
whoa.

JJ1347 will be known in
   every server,
every chat,
every story
ever told
about the night
the Sandbox developers
accidentally destroyed
twenty million avatars
but not ours.

She is legend.

And she is about to get fired.

JORDAN J

<JORDANJMAGEDDON!!!>

Holy shiitake mushrooms, holy shirtballs, holy baby Cheez-Its, holy everything in the world I cannot believe what I am seeing and hearing except I have to believe it because Ben B just pulled up a message board on his phone and the whole world, like the whole actual world is going crazy about the mystery new Ghostkiller who saved four avatars in a one-person stand that lasted all night. I mean I guess it turns out that grown-ups CAN actually learn how to play Sandbox and do a really good job at it even if they walk into walls for the first week.

▫ ▫ ▫ ▫

We are having to try super super super extra hard to be quiet out here because there is a Very Serious Grown-Up meeting happening in the other room but omg omg omg Ms J is so famous now and she saved us! She saved us all! While we were working so hard to try to save her! And now we're here and we can hear some of the words in the Very Serious Grown-Up meeting because the principal's office door is almost shut but not all the way shut and she is saying things like *regardless of that* and *you took them off of school property* and then a bunch of words we can't hear and that's when I realize duh duh duh, this is the moment we got ourselves prepped and ready for why are we just sitting here and Ben B must figure that out at the same time I do because he shakes his paper at everyone and says, *Come on you y'alls! This is what we came to do. She saved us, now let's go save her.*

□ □ □ □

And so we all flip open our books and march in.

□ □ □ □

[fart noise]

(For good luck.)

BEN B

<BenBee>

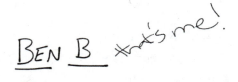

<u>BEN B</u> ~~that~~ it's me!

As you make your way through the fields of fire you realize night is falling and ghosts will soon abound. But what lies beyond the fields of fire? You have been trudging forward for days. The future is so close, nearly in your grasp. It's getting dark, though. What should you do?

If you build a quick shelter and rest for the night,
turn to **page 145**.

If you keep moving forward, turn to **page 150**.

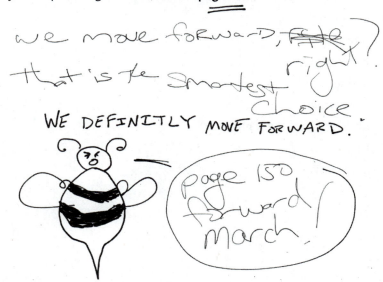

we move forward, ~~the~~ right?

that is the smartest choice.

WE DEFINITLY MOVE FORWARD.

page 150 forward march!

Ms. J.
My teacher.
Our teacher.
Only for
this super short
summer school
time,

but

so many things
she's taught me
have stuck
in my mind,
like seeds
in a garden
and I can feel them growing
making my brain bigger
every day,

making me proud
and smart
and happy
and good—

that's why
we always
move forward.

Ben Y.
Turn to page 150.

Oh, also . . .

I AM DIVERGENT!

BEN Y

<0BenwhY>

BEN Y

You are surely brave, but sometimes bravery comes at a cost. As you press forward, dodging flames that grow larger and taller, you become surrounded by ghosts. You will need to make a sacrifice.

If you sacrifice someone in your rag-tag group of "allies", turn to **page 148**.

If you sacrifice ur self, turn to **page 175**.

do i have 2 do finger quotes when i say "allies"?

ONLY IF YOU WANT TO.

PAGE 175!

y do i always look like this in ur drawings?

YOU'RE A FIERCE FLORIDA PANTHER. THEY ARE REALLY HARD TO DRAW! ‿

Ms. J, you probably already
    know this
because you can read minds
    sometimes,
but just in case you don't,
I want you to know,
I figured out you hurt my
    feelings .
because you were clueless
not because you were unkind,
and even though that still sort
    of sucks,
I think you finally heard me,
when I freaked out.
I think you finally saw me, too.
And I'm sorry I yelled like that,
but I'm not sorry I opened
    your eyes,

and I hope you know
that I can see you now,
the real you,
the sacrifices you've made
to be a good teacher
and to be
whatever the word is
for a good teacher-friend.

Jordan J.
Please turn to page 175.

And . . .

I AM DIVERGENT!

JORDAN J

<JORDANJMAGEDDON!!!>

i will read it in my Spartacus (the dog s of the movie guy)

No one's sacrifice will ever be in vain and u build a great statue to honor your fallen friend. While mining jewels to decorate this monument, u are approached by a dirty pig farmer begging for some of the jewels so he can sell them to help fee his pigs.

If you give the farmer some jewels, turn to **page 173**.

If you ignore the farmer, turn to **page 164**.

page! 173

voice
so that
it will be
super
extra
perfectly
great.
MAYBE JUST
READ IT IN
YOUR REGULAR
VOICE?

Ms. J (same name! No relation.) would have a really fantastic statue if we all built one for her because it would look like an awesome stingray, but with bright colors and fancy earrings and big hair and we would need all the jewels in all of Sandbox to make the statue's smile as sparkly as Ms. J's smile is and of course we would all give the farmer some jewels because we are all kind people and maybe the most important summer school lesson any of us learned is that it's good to be able to read out loud, and it's good to be able to make pork chops in Sandbox (or at least try really hard to do that, right Ms. J?) but really, the most important thing of all is to be kind and sometimes you think you're being kind but you're not and so you have to learn to listen to people when they tell you how to do a better job and then you have to do a better job. We all learned how to do a lot of better jobs at a lot of things and so Ms. J should be able to keep her job because her job is to teach us how to do all those better jobs and she's done a really good job of doing that. Javier, can you please go to page 173, please.

Aaaand, I AM DIVERGENT!

JAVIER

`<jajajavier:)>`

B-B-Ben B is g-going to
    h-h-help me.
I hope th-th-that's o-k-k-kay.

Ready, B-B-Ben B?

Do you know the k-k-key of C?
Do you know Johnny
    C-C-Cash's song "Ring
    of F-F-Fire"?

C-cool.
Okay.

Go.

LET'S DO THIS!

The farmer takes the jewels you gave him and he eats them. This surprises you because jewels are not meant to be food. The farmer's belly lights up, beautiful colors swirling together until they shoot from his fingertips, from his eyes, from his nose, from his mouth. He is no pig farmer! He is not even a he! The Goddess of Sand stands before you, glowing so bright you have to look away.

She says, "Your kindness proves you are a true winner in all things. Yes, you have worked hard to save your server and save yourself, but you have not forgotten to help save others, too. I have a reward for you. Which of these boxes would you like?"

If you choose the gold box, turn to **page 172**.

If you choose the black box, turn to **page 171**.

you can do it!

I CAN DO IT
I CAN DO IT
I CAN DO IT

U can do it, javier!

you can do it, man!

322

CHAT

Divergent Dingleberries

Private server created by: **BenBee**

Password required

Avatar name:

Password:

IMPORTANT MESSAGE ABOUT GHOST SEASON: Please contact customer service if you were affected by the bug in update OS 1.5.1. The volume of calls and correspondence is extremely high, so your patience is appreciated.

BenBee: So what I'm trying to understand is

BenBee: we spent this whole time building a pyramid we didn't need?

BenBee: because Ms. J knew the Ghostkiller potion???????

BenBee: how??????????

0BenwhY: I taught it to her

jajajavier:): No, I taught it to her!

JORDANJMAGEDDON!!!: No, I taught it to her!

BenBee: har har everyone's hilarious

0BenwhY: for real, though, I taught it to her.

0BenwhY: My brother invented it and he taught me just before he died

0BenwhY: hello?

0BenwhY: I can see you're all still here

BenBee: so wait, what? The original Ghostkiller was...

0BenwhY: my brother, Benicio. He was also the original Ben Y.

BenBee: So he's not a legend, then? I mean, he IS a legend, but not a fake, uh, you know what I mean, right? Wow, I'm really sorry—

CHAT INFRACTION

BenBee: I never thought ghostkiller could actually be real, but

OBenwhY: he was actually my brother

BenBee: why didn't you tell us?

OBenwhY: it's not really something I like to talk about.

BenBee: oh. ok.
BenBee: I'm really sorry. About your brother and about doubting him and you and all that

OBenwhY: thanks, Ben B.

JORDANJMAGEDDON!!!: 😪 🖤

jajajavier:): ((((((((((((((((obenwhy))))))))))))))))

OBenwhY: thanks everybody.
OBenwhY: so, can we talk about Ms. J totally OWNING that ghostkiller potion? omg

0BenwhY: officially more ghost kills than Benecio! In one night!

JORDANJMAGEDDON!!!: I saw her on the actual real TV news last night and thank goodness i couldn't choke on ice cream cause I woul--

CHAT INFRACTION

JORDANJMAGEDDON!!!: d have

JJ11347 ENTERS GAME

JJ11347: Hello, hello, hello! How are you all doing?

JORDANJMAGEDDON!!!: how did you like our reading? wasn't Javier amazzzzzzzzing??

jajajavier:): 😊 i was only amazzzzzzzing because of all you y'alls.

JORDANJMAGEDDON!!!: 😄 😊

BenBee: How are YOU doing, Ms. J? Are you still our teacher?

JORDANJMAGEDDON!!!: 🙏

JJ11347: Well, I have good news and bad news.

OBenwhY: son of a bench, we actually got you fired, didn't we? i am so so so so sorry. i will never win a race again, I---

CHAT INFRACTION

OBenwhY: will always open doors slowly. I am so so so so so sorry.

JJ11347: Hold on a second. I did not get fired.

JORDANJMAGEDDON!!!: 🐧

BenBee: 🎉
jajajavier:): 🎉

OBenwhY: 🎉 🎉 🎉

JJ11347: That's the good news.
JJ11347: The sort of, but overall not really, bad news is that I have been reassigned.
JJ11347: No more room 113.
JJ11347: Administration didn't like it that I took you all off campus. To the willow tree.
JJ11347: I didn't have permission from them or from your parents.

OBenwhY: How is the willow tree NOT on campus?

JJ11347: Right?! Well, it turns out it's not. And that earned me the assessment.

JJ11347: After the assessment went . . . awry . . . well, you y'alls know what happened.

JJ11347: And now, no more room 113.

OBenwhY: NOOOOO

JJ11347: But! I've been moved back to the library!

JJ11347: Administration seems to think they can keep a better eye on me there

JJ11347: I'm not sure they realize that librarians cause more trouble than ANYONE. 😈

JJ11347: I'm actually quite excited about the move

JJ11347: and I am expecting you all to visit me in the library

JJ11347: a lot

jajajavier:): I guess you're going to need to order a lot more Many Choices Sandbox Adventure books, huh?

CHAT INFRACTION

BenBee: Maybe there could be a typing club in the library

JORDANJMAGEDDON!!!: typing club? 👇

JORDANJMAGEDDON!!!: oh, unless you mean for

JORDANJMAGEDDON!!!: typing practice? 😜

0BenwhY: I could definitely use more typing practice

jajajavier:): Really, there is never enough typing practice, if you ask me.

JJ11347: Haha, you all are too much.
JJ11347: A typing club sounds like a great idea

BenBee: You mean a divergent idea?

JJ11347: Maybe we should call it the Divergent Typing Practice Club.

0BenwhY: That is a terrible name. 😄

BenBee: Anyone interested in finally finishing this pyramid? Just for fun?
BenBee: Hello?
BenBee: where are you going? throw me a fairy so I can catch up.
BenBee: holy shirtballs, is that what I think it is?
BenBee: I totally forgot it was here!
BenBee: the accidental chickenfall!
BenBee: my best creation ever

JJ11347: I don't know.
JJ11347: I kind of think the Dingleberry server was your best creation ever.

JORDANJMAGEDDON!!!: holy shiitake mushrooms, you know what I just figured out?

JORDANJMAGEDDON!!!: Ms. J saved our server and we saved ourselves

JORDANJMAGEDDON!!!: we made the book come true!

JORDANJMAGEDDON!!!: does that happen with EVERY book you read to the end?

JORDANJMAGEDDON!!!: can we read Tips and Tricks to Winning Fierce Across America next?

JORDANJMAGEDDON!!!: ????????????????????????????

OBenwhY: Maybe let's read Divergent Nerds Surviving Seventh Grade next.

BenBee: Is that an actual book?

jajajavier:): Give me a fresh notebook, some new pens, and the rest of the summer.

JORDANJMAGEDDON!!!: 😜

JORDANJMAGEDDON!!!: I bet Ms. J will even put it in the library.

JJ11347: 😜 Maybe I will.

JJ11347: Sorry to chat and run, but I have a library to get in order.

BenBee: High five and bye, for now, Ms. J.

JORDANJMAGEDDON!!!: 🖐 🖐 & bye!

jajajavier:): high five and bye!

OBenwhY: high five and bye, Ms. J. It's good to have you back.

JJ11347: High five and bye, you y'alls. I'll see you soon. And don't forget to keep reading for the rest of the summer. Reading is—

CHAT INFRACTION
JJ11347 HAS BEEN EJECTED FROM GAME
THIRTY MINUTE RESPAWN COUNTDOWN BEGINS NOW

Florida Rigorous Academic Assessment Test
Summary Report—Language Arts Test Performance

BenBee	

				3	4
Basic Understandir					x
Comprehension of					x
Analysis and Eval					x
Understanding o Grammar and P					x

It has been a joy to get to know you, Ben B. BenBee is quite a fellow, too. Thank you for showing me that I can always learn something new and that you point a pickax down and not sideways.

Kind Human Being Assessment Test

	1	2	3	4
Diamond mining				x
Creative planning				x
Instructing others with patience and kindness				x
Leadership in the face of tight Ghost Season deadline				x

Exceeds ALL STANDARDS of being a brilliant and kind human being.

SEMESTER COMMENTS

Recommendations:

- Keep typing!
- Visit the library a LOT
  when school starts.

KEY	
4	Exceeds Standards
3	Meets Standards
2	Working Toward Standards
1	Not Meeting Standards
N/A	Not Assessed

100% DIVERGENT

FLORIDA UNIFIED SCHOOL DISTRICT
Florida Department of Education

TEACHER EVAULATION

Teacher's Name: _____ SSN: _____

School: _____ Year: _____

Meets Standards	Needs Improvement	Below Standards	EVALUATION CRITERIA
			I. Planning/Preparation
○	○	○	Plans for students at all instructional levels.
			II. Learning Environment
○	○	○	Creates a warm and inviting environment.
○	○	○	Encourages higher level critical thinking skills.
○	○	○	Involves students at all instructional levels.
○	○	○	Practices fairness and consistency in matters of student discipline.
			III. Quality of Instruction
○	○	○	Communicates material clearly and effectively.
○	○	○	Maximizes use of time and student involvement.
○	○	○	Provides prompt and constructive feedbacl.
○	○	○	Utilizes assessment tools to adapt to and adjust student instruction.
○	○	○	Encourages higher level critical thinking skills.
○	○	○	Performs in way that leads to measurable growth in students.

Grade 6 Exit Level

Florida Rigorous Academic Assessment Test
Summary Report—Language Arts Test Performance

OBenwhY					

				3	4
Basic Understandir					x
Comprehension of					x
Analysis and Evalua					x
Understanding of an Grammar and Punctu					x

My life will be forever changed by knowing you, Ben Y. Your passion for everything, from fashion to sandbox to speaking your mind is an inspiration. Also, I really appreciate the potion recipe. WOW.

Kind Human Being Assessment Test

	1	2	3	4
Fairy ~~pooping~~ popping				x
Potion creating				x
Teamwork skills				x
Insturcting others with patience and kindness				x

Exceeds ALL STANDARDS of being an exceptionally smart and kind human being.

SEMESTER COMMENTS

Recommendations:

• Continue to shine!

• Visit the library a LOT when school starts.

KEY	
4	Exceeds Standards
3	Meets Standards
2	Working Toward Standards
1	Not Meeting Standards
N/A	Not Assessed

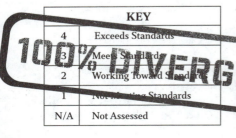

100% DIVERGENT

FLORIDA UNIFIED SCHOOL DISTRICT

Florida Department of Education

TEACHER EVAULATION

Teacher's Name: _____ ms j _____

SSL: _____ beny _____

School: _____

Year: _____ Summer school _____

You are the best teacher I've ever had thank you for being great even if it took a minute for you to see me Also T-y for killing so many ghosts one you are so fine holy shit balls

Meets Standards	Needs Improvement	Below Standards	EVALUATION CRITERIA
			I. Planning/Preparation
⊗	○	○	Plans for students at all instructional levels.
			II. Learning Environment
⊗	○	○	Creates a warm and inviting environment.
⊗	○	○	Encourages higher level critical thinking skills.
⊗	○	○	Involves students at all instructional levels.
⊗	○	○	Practices fairness and consistency in matters of student discipline.
			III. Quality of Instruction
⊗	○	○	Communicates material clearly and effectively.
⊗	○	○	Maximizes use of time and student involvement.
⊗	○	○	Provides prompt and constructive feedbacl.
⊗	○	○	Utilizes assessment tools to adapt to and adjust student instruction.
⊗	○	○	Encourages higher level critical thinking skills.
⊗	○	○	Performs in way that leads to measurable growth in students.

Grade 6 Exit Level

Florida Rigorous Academic Assessment Test
Summary Report—Language Arts Test Performance

JORDANJMAGEDDON!!!

			3	4
Basic Unders				x
Comprehens				x
Analysis and				x
Understandi Grammar an				x

[handwritten note overlapping table:] Every day you teach me a new way to see the world, Jordan J (no relation). You fill me with wonder at the way your incredible brain sees every moment in such a magical way. How I envy you, and how lucky I am to also be a Jordan Jackson.

Kin ... Test

	1	2	3	4
Heavy lifting				x
Staying on task despite chat infractions				x
Protecting others				x
Instructing others with patience and kindness				

Exceeds ALL STANDARDS of being an exceptionally gifted and kind human being.

SEMESTER COMMENTS

Recommendations:

- Keep dancing!
- Visit the library a LOT when school starts.

KEY	
4	Exceeds Standards
3	Meets Standards
2	Working Toward Standards
1	Not Meeting Standards
N/A	Not Assessed

100% DIVERGENT

FLORIDA UNIFIED SCHOOL DISTRICT
Florida Department of Education

Jordan Jackson,
Summer-school

ssaualosaub (Superteam awsome)

TEACHER EVAULATION

Jordan Jackson!!

Teacher's Name: *Jordan Jackson!!!*   SSN: *Awsome summer*

School: *Hi-Five!!!*   Year: *assessing You* ✗

Meets Standards	Needs Improvement	Below Standards	EVALUATION CRITERIA
			I. Planning/Preparation
∅	E	S	Plans for students at all instructional levels.
			II. Learning Environment *Never too Hot or cold*
A	A+	A+	Creates a warm and inviting environment.
∅	O	O%	Encourages higher level critical thinking skills.
(-)	C	S	Involves students at all instructional levels.
∅	E	S	Practices fairness and consistency in matters of student discipline.
			III. Quality of Instruction
A+	A+	A+	Communicates material clearly and effectively.
∅	∅	O	Maximizes use of time and student involvement.
✗	E	S	Provides prompt and constructive feedbacl.
A	+	+	Utilizes assessment tools to adapt to and adjust student instruction.
∅	∅	O	Encourages higher level critical thinking skills.

I have grown one whole inch this summer A+

Performs in way that leads to measurable growth in students.

Jordan Jackson + Jordan Jackson!! Superteam awsome

Florida Rigorous Academic Assessment Test
Summary Report—Language Arts Test Performance

jajajavier:)

				4
Basic Understanding				x
Comprehension of L				x
Analysis and Evaluat				x
Understanding of an Grammar and Punct				x

My enigma, my tutor, my foil, my friend. I learn something new from you every day. Javier, your creativity, your resilience, your stubborness are impressive and enviable. I look forward to watching you take over the world, one stroke of your pen at a time.

Kind Human Being Assessment Test

	1	2	3	4
Learning to trust others				x
Creative ideas				x
Uniting all players regardless of skill				x
Instructing others with patience and kindness				x

Exceeds ALL STANDARDS of being a brilliant an incredibly talented and kind human being.

SEMESTER COMMENTS

Recommendations:

• Keep drawing!

• Visit the library a LOT when school starts.

KEY	
4	Exceeds Standards
3	Meets Standards
2	Working Toward Standards
1	Not Meeting Standards
N/A	Not Assessed

100% DIVERGENT

FLORIDA UNIFIED SCHOOL DISTRICT
Florida Department of Education

TEACHER EVAULATION

Teacher's Name: _Ms J_   SSN: _Javier Jimnez_

School: _____   _summer_

Meets Standards	Needs Improvement	Below Standards	EVALUATION CRITERIA
			I. Planning/Preparation
○	○	○	Plans for students at all instructional levels.
			II. Learning Environment
○	○	○	Creates a warm and inviting environment.
○	○	○	Encourages higher level critical thinking skills.
○	○	○	Involves students at all instructional levels.
○	○	○	Practices fairness and consistency in matters of student discipline.
			III. Quality of Instruction
○	○	○	Communicates material clearly and effectively.
○	○	○	Maximizes use of time and student involvement.
○	○	○	Provides prompt and constructive feedbacl.
○	○	○	Utilizes assessment tools to adapt to and adjust student instruction.
○	○	○	Encourages higher level critical thinking skills.
○	○	○	Performs in way that leads to measurable growth in students.

PICTURED: BEST TEACHER* EVER!

* Stingray/Ghost Killer

ABOUT THE AUTHOR

K.A. Holt
lives in Austin, Texas.
Her most favorite thing in the world,
other than embarrassing her kids,
is to write books
that may or may not
embarrass imaginary kids.

Also by K.A. Holt

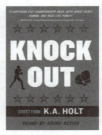